THE LANGUAGE OF FLOWERS

FROM THIS DAY FORWARD

BOOK 1

DARA GIRARD

ILORI
Press Books, LLC

ISBN: 978-1-949764642

The Language of Flowers

Published by ILORI Press Books

Cover design by ILORI Press Books

Cover Photo © ivonnewierink/depositphotos

This is a work of fiction. Names, characters, places and incidents are either the product of the author's imagination or are used fictitiously, and any resemblance to actual persons, living or dead is entirely coincidental.

ILORI PRESS BOOKS, LLC

P.O. Box 10332

Silver Spring, MD 20914

www.iloripressbooks.com

BOOKS BY DARA GIRARD

Duvall Sisters

The Glass Slipper Project

Taming Mariella

A Reluctant Hero

The Black Stockings Society

Power Play

A Gentleman's Offer

Body Chemistry

Round the Clock

Return of the Black Stockings Society

Playing for Keeps

After Hours

A Private Affair

Just One Look

Private Lessons

The Main Attraction

Ladies of the Pen

Words of Seduction

Pages of Passion

Beneath the Covers

Henson Series

Table for Two

Gaining Interest

Careless Rapture

Dangerous Curves

Familiar Stranger

It Happened One Wedding

Unexpected Pleasure

Midnight Promise

Sweet Temptation

Always and Forever

Truly Yours

Say Yes

Picture Perfect

By My Side

Clifton Sisters

The Sapphire Pendant

The Amber Stone

The Emerald Ring

Fortune Brothers

A Tempting Proposal

A Seductive Arrangement

An Unforgettable Moment

Novels

Honest Betrayal

The Daughters of Winston Barnett

Remember My Name

Illusive Flame

Winterwood Lane

Promise Me

This Changes Everything

Sparks

Piece of Cake

Best Laid Plans

Her Tender Touch

Dream of Me

1

A PITY TOSS.

Everyone standing outside the church door knew what was about to happen.

Only the bride's wedding gown, as she stood at the top of the concrete steps, distinguished the event from looking like a fashion show with fifty or so guests dressed in custom tailored, form fitted outfits that could have sprung from the pages of *Ovation* magazine or the latest Nollywood movie.

Gold, pink, green and silver geles and hats rising high to blue sky like a sea of flowers and butterflies with outstretched wings as they anxiously waited for the bride's next move.

Someone coughed but the roar of a motorcycle making its way through the large, crowded parking lot behind them, muffled the sound. The smell of exhaust mingled with the heavy scent of newly cut grass.

The moment the bouquet flew in the air, the humidity of the Maryland spring day seeming to hold it still as if to give everyone time to part, they all knew their role.

Only one person was meant to catch it. They needed to

make room for her. Heaven forbid anyone else accidentally did so. The bouquet was meant for one person only.

The bride's unmarried, thirty-seven year old sister.

The unemployed one.

The "other daughter" who Mr. Kayode had kindly given his name.

The short, chubby one who had the audacity to show up in —not the richly laced, golden and red colored aso-ebi to distinguish the bride's family—but a similar colored ankhara styled dress she'd *worn before* (!!) at a naming ceremony.

She'd told anyone who'd listen that the expensive fabric the bride had chosen was out of her budget and she wasn't going to spend money she didn't have or charge it, which was also heresy because half the guests had done exactly that. Every sane person with good taste and breeding knew it was much better to go into debt and keep up appearances than to shame your family or yourself.

But Maya Kayode lacked those two crucial traits, which was not Mr. Kayode's fault since he'd generously married a woman with a child and raised her as his own.

Nor was it Mrs. Kayode's fault since everyone knew Maya was nothing like her other three daughters.

Few worried about Gwen, the eldest of the Kayode children, the bride, who'd gone to a top university and worked in finance.

The distinction became important in the case of the other two. No one wanted to make the mistake and confuse Maya with the two other unmarried Kayode sisters.

There was obedient Ava, as sweet as her caramel colored skin, who was thankfully (Praise God!) engaged, and then dear Catherine, who was so rail thin and homely, with skin as lackluster as dried leaves. The family had designated her to care for the parents until their deaths, in which case she'd be expected to live with one of the sisters and help look after their children (heaven forbid she would foolishly think to have a single life of her own).

But there was a minor hope for Maya.

She was pretty enough, with rich chocolate brown skin, full lips, great breeding hips (what else were hips that size for?) and whose expiration date was a couple years off, although her smooth complexion could fool a man to think it may be closer to a decade.

Marriage must be on her horizon.

The bouquet was meant for her. She wouldn't have to fight for the assortment of red garden roses, blush pink mums and purple spray roses. It would sail in her direction. All she had to do was catch it.

The only problem was Maya didn't want it.

Aside from not understanding such a silly and superstitious ritual, Maya had warned her sister, Gwen, not to toss it at her. She didn't want the attention. It was bad enough that she knew her outfit would stand out and make her the black sheep of the family. But on top of that, to be singled out with pity on her sister's special day was too much.

She'd told her—pleaded, begged, warned—numerous times, each time with more force.

"I mean it. Don't even look in my direction. I don't want it," Maya told Gwen only two weeks ago in Gwen's apartment while helping her pack her living room items to donate to a relative since she'd no longer need many of the things now that she was moving into her new house.

"Sure, sure," Gwen'd said with a long sigh and rolling her eyes.

But clearly her sister hadn't listened to a single word. Which wasn't unusual since Gwen didn't hear what she didn't want to.

Briefly, Maya thought of rushing up the stairs and tackling her. But then she might end up tearing her sister's glass-beaded twenty thousand dollar dress and then she'd need to escape and enter the witness protection program.

Maya then considered catching the bouquet, holding it high above her head with a big smile while everyone cheered, before she dropped the offending flowers to the ground and proceeded to stomp on them. Not once but ten times (deep breaths, count to ten one school counselor had told her after she'd been labeled a child with "anger issues") mashing each petal with cruel delight under the sole of her heels. She'd take her fury out on the sleek petals, crushing them.

She could imagine people staring, gaping in horror. Most would likely say, "This is why you're not married! Do you think any man would want you?"

And such comments—told to her *ad nauseam*—would only make her want to smash the bouquet more. Why was she seen as deficient just because she didn't have a man? She didn't want one, at least not yet. She'd had one and he hadn't improved her life much. No matter how much people had congratulated her on a good catch (he'd been a college dean from a good family who thought her art was "cute") she'd felt lonely.

It felt better to be alone than with someone who didn't understand her. Who thought she needed to be fixed somehow. She didn't feel as if her life was missing something. Especially not a husband. But the sight of the bouquet also offended her for another reason that had nothing to do with matrimony.

The bouquet twisted her stomach in knots because she hated flowers.

With a passion.

Every important turning point in her life that had brought disaster, sadness or both had started with flowers.

She remembered the scent of the peonies when she'd been

left in a hotel lobby when her mother forgot her. She remembered the kindly clerk and the police officer who'd smelled like sweat and coffee but was also very patient.

She remembered red rose petals littering the foyer of their cramped apartment when her mother dashed off into the evening with the man who'd brought them, instead of staying home with Maya, even though she'd told her mother she was scared.

"There's nothing to be scared of," her mother had told her with an impatient sigh as she put on her earrings. "Go to sleep."

"But I'm not tired."

"Keep the TV on for company or go online." She glanced at the man then said in a low voice, "I'm doing this for both of us."

Maya didn't know what she meant and her mother never cared to explain. But all she knew was her mother preferred getting flowers over being with her.

But Maya's hatred of flowers didn't solidify until her grandmother's passing. Her grandmother had been the one person who loved her. A Nigerian immigrant who'd arrived in the US as a woman in her late forties with a broken heart over the death of her beloved husband, nursing skills, and a rebellious sixteen-year-old daughter. She had a son who'd left Nigeria before his father's passing to study engineering in Canada and had decided to settle there.

Through working odd jobs and taking courses to allow her to practice nursing in her new country, she'd managed to make a life for herself and her daughter, proudly buying a small pillbox home to settle in during retirement.

Maya had gone to live with the dark skinned, white haired woman at five years old when her mother was struggling with life (no one got more specific than that). She only knew that nine years later she was living with her mother again and three new half-sisters.

And all because her grandmother had collapsed in her garden—splayed out in the flower bed—after weeding her gardenias.

Maya remembered keeping her hands in a tight fist during the entire funeral as she glared at the abundant flowers surrounding the casket, hating their scent, their bright colors, inwardly thinking: The flowers killed her. If she hadn't been in that damn garden tending to the roses, looking after the tulips and those stupid gardenias, she would still be alive. Flowers were selfish, taking up so much of her time and energy Maya never knew why her grandmother enjoyed toiling so much.

That day flowers not only signaled disaster and sadness but also loss. Loss of a family she'd known, loss of the familiar, loss of a love that had felt safe and comforting.

The final event that fueled her flower hatred had been a bouquet she had received for her graduation from university. That bouquet came with the scent of betrayal: A sickeningly sweet scent with the sting of a withering slow death. Maya didn't know if the flowers had been picked too soon or too late but some of the buds never opened while those that managed to, barely pried open before they sagged and died.

They were a gift from her best friend.

The best friend who would later steal her dissertation and then accuse her of theft.

The best friend who would go out with the guy Maya had a crush on just because she could (Maya had asked her why). The best—or rather former best—friend who was now happily tenured at a prestigious university and hadn't caught a sexually transmitted infection (or several) and fallen through a manhole and disappeared as Maya had often wished.

No, she hated flowers. Detested them and she had every right to.

Her sister knew that.

And Maya had warned her.

But Gwen, like everyone else, thought her distain for flowers was silly. Infantile. Perhaps it was, but it wouldn't change the fact that she wasn't going to catch the bouquet.

Perhaps if she had, the toss of the bouquet wouldn't have turned into a fiasco spoken about for generations.

Perhaps if she had gritted her teeth and just taken the humiliation, as she'd grown accustomed to doing, she wouldn't have nearly killed a man.

And not just any man.

The one person she despised more than flowers.

2

———

To BE fair she hadn't been aiming for him (as some people later suggested). She hadn't been aiming for anyone. Her only goal had been to avoid the bouquet.

So she'd quickly ducked and ran like a woman who took pride in the self-defense class she'd completed. Self-preservation at all cost. Don't be afraid to look silly. That's all she thought as she pushed people out of the way. She didn't even realize she'd hit him hard enough that he'd lost his balance and stumbled back into the parking lot (she'd told her sister it had been dangerous to do the toss there) and gotten hit by an SUV.

He actually bounced.

She never knew a body could bounce like that. But he had bounced off the SUV that had abruptly halted—too late, leaving the screech of tires and scent of burning rubber hanging in the air—and hit the parked limo ready to take the newlyweds to the reception—before his lanky, lean frame slid to the ground like a deflating balloon.

For the longest moment it felt as if no one moved. As if it hadn't really happened. Maya remembered the buzzing of a bee that had been attracted to the now forgotten bouquet left on the ground like a disregarded football.

She heard a car door slam close, heels on the asphalt then a scream. "Oh my God! Oh my God!"

Maya shifted her gaze to the young driver-a woman barely twenty-who'd emerged from the SUV. Her cry of distress forced everyone out of their shared paralysis.

There was no need to ask if there was a doctor. The event was a Nigerian-American wedding so there were at least three to call on (plus a resident, two LPNs and three RNs).

Maya was still trying to process what had just happened when she felt a big whack on the back of her head. "What have you done?" her mother said, her accent thick with anger.

Maya briefly saw stars before she glared at the handbag in her mother's hand. She pointed at it. "Admit it! You keep rocks in there, don't you?"

Her mother's eyes widened. "You want to make fun?" She hit Maya on the side of the head this time with just her hand, which wasn't much better. Maya swore her mother's hands were large enough to palm a bowling ball. She rubbed the side of her head. "No."

Her mother raised her hands and gazed to the sky as if in praise. "Thank All Mighty God his parents left early so they don't have to see this disaster." Her hands fell to her side and she glared at Maya. "I can't believe you did this."

"I didn't do anything," Maya said offended by the accusation. "At least not on purpose."

"You have ruined your sister's wedding." Whack! "You have shamed us." Whack!

Maya held up her hands to block the next blow. "Enough."

"I'll decide when it's enough."

Her mother lifted her hand to strike another well placed blow but Maya grabbed her wrist. "No, you won't."

Her mother snatched her hand away. "Eh eh look at those eyes. The dark eyes of your father. Will you assault me too? Will I be your next victim?"

Maya hated when her mother compared her to a man she'd never met. There were only two pictures of him at a party a friend of her mother had hosted but they were a little blurry. However, from what little she could gather from her mother's description he had cold eyes, a cruel mouth and big build. She'd once asked her mother if he was so awful why she'd slept with him and that had gotten Maya enough whacks that she'd never asked again.

"That's not fair," Maya said, taking a step back to keep proper distance between them. "I didn't hit him."

"You pushed him into the road."

"It was an accident."

Her mother shoved her forward. "Go."

"Where?"

"Go and help."

Maya looked at the crowd surrounding the fallen man. She couldn't even see him. "They don't need my help."

"At least show that you're worried," her mother said with another shove. "Cry if you need to."

"I don't feel like crying."

Her mother's voice turned so cold Maya shivered half expecting snow to start falling. "I can make you cry."

It wasn't an empty threat. Maya held up her hands in surrender. "I'm going. I'm going." She hurried over to the crowd. But there hadn't been much progress. Her nemesis, Keeden Adesina, remained on the ground while a number of people recorded the incident on their cell phones, others took pictures (some of the fallen man but mostly of themselves in front of him) and the three doctors argued over the best approach.

Not about which hospital to send him.

Not about the right choice of action to take.

But rather who had more seniority. Who had the right seniority to offer advice in the first place. The names of Ivy League colleges and top residencies were thrown about, travels and patient records—basically oral CVs which had no place in an emergency.

Which was always a problem when there was too much ego, intellect and not enough sense.

Maya felt a nudge in the side and looked up at The Old Woman. Lena Olawu was really only fourteen but she looked sixteen with her shoulder length black wig (she owned more wigs than a drag queen, which was no surprise since Lena's mother owned enough for two) and form fitted blue dress and silver tinted contacts plus she acted much older.

Some kids had an old soul. This one was possibly from another galaxy. She also happened to be one of Keeden's favorite cousins. Maya tried her best not to hold it against her. "Do something," Lena said, her eyes pleading for help. "They won't listen to me." She looked scared which she rarely did. This wasn't the time to worry about protocol, tradition and hierarchy. She'd apologize tomorrow.

Maya stepped forward and raised her voice over the crowd and said, "Who has called an ambulance?"

3

———

THE DOCTORS STOPPED BICKERING, the sound of the camera clicks fell silent and everyone looked at her as if she'd spoken in tongues.

Maya rolled her eyes and silently swore. She hated the man but this was bad. "You must be joking. You all have your cell phones out but no one thought to use it to call an ambulance?"

"I thought she was going to do it," one guest said.

"I thought he said he would," another added.

"His condition is stable," the two nurses said then preceded to tell her, in varying accounts (volleying like a ball in a tennis match), that he didn't appear to have anything broken, the first preliminary observation was sound. Maya thanked them—silently thankful a few people had sense—then pulled out her cell phone. "Now I'll call an ambulance."

Doctor Such and Such adjusted his tie. "He must go to—"

"It doesn't matter where he goes," Maya said trying her best to keep her tone respectful, although she presently thought the person was an idiot. "He needs to go to a hospital. Any hospital."

"No." This one word came from the prone man. The man whose eyes were closed but whose words were spoken with such fierce command it silenced them both.

Keeden opened his eyes and glared at her. Just her! As if he blamed her for everything, and said, "I don't need one." He started to rise, but one of the nurses forced him back down.

"Don't move," the nurse said. Considering he was built like a ram, Keeden had no option but to keep still.

"I don't need an ambulance," Keeden said, his pain soaked voice belying his words. "Such fuss. I'm fine."

"You hit your head."

"I think he hit more than just his head," Doctor So and So said adjusting her glasses.

"There could be internal bleeding," Doctor Such and Such said clearing his throat.

Maya looked over at the young driver who'd managed to be subdued by her cousin. Cousin Jules, the one who could convince you to give him a kidney and persuade you that he was doing you a favor. The cousin with the welcoming grin and soft hands. It was a dangerous situation, but she was too preoccupied to warn her. She'd find out soon enough or she'd tell Jules to let her be later. He wasn't the main focus now.

"If someone doesn't get him off the ground in thirty seconds," Maya said. "I'm calling an ambulance."

"Come here," Keeden said.

She hesitated, unsure he'd spoken. He lay as still as a statue with his eyes closed again. He looked almost peaceful.

"Now," he repeated.

He didn't sound peaceful. The tone made the hairs on the nape of her neck rise. She didn't like taking orders from him, but people were looking and he was injured...so she pushed down her temper and bent over him. "Yes?"

"Closer."

She knelt beside him, glad she'd worn an outfit with enough give that getting off the ground wouldn't be awkward, and tilted her head close to his mouth.

He grabbed her wrist, his palm like fire against her skin, and said in a voice that dripped with venom, in a tone so soft only she could hear him, "Call an ambulance and you'll be the one who needs it."

Two threats in one day. How thrilling.

She tried to twist her wrist free. "What do you have against--?"

"I'm not kidding."

His eyes remained closed but, damn him, he frightened her a little. She didn't like being frightened of anyone. Especially him. Humor was her best defense. She tried harder to loosen his hold. "If you keep flirting like this I might get the wrong idea."

His grip tightened enough to cause tears to spring to her eyes. The bastard was still strong. He had enough life in him yet. Or if he was dying he was determined to drag her down with him. "I mean it," he said.

"Okay. Okay."

He opened his eyes. Dark, probing eyes filled with anger but also hazy with pain. "Promise."

And his voice had weakened too. It was no longer as fierce as it had been only moments before. It caused her heart to shift in sympathy. The thought revolted her. She didn't want to feel anything for this man, let alone sympathy. Compassion was wasted on someone like him, but, to her annoyance, she hated seeing anyone in pain.

He may not want an ambulance but he needed care.

She bit her nails into his arm, causing him to wince and release her. "No, I'd never promise you anything," she said, trying to regain her composure as she rubbed where his hand had been, angered that it still felt hot from his touch, "but I won't call anyone. It's your life hanging in the balance not mine." She quickly rose to her feet before he could reply.

She pointed to Doctor Such and Such. She was their best hope, she worked at the nearest hospital, she wasn't the most senior but she was good at following directions when it was put in an authoritative tone. She was basically a pleaser. Maya needed that now. Someone who wouldn't argue. "You take him," she said. Before there was an outcry she asked the nurse to go with Doctor So and So because when the nurse reached his full height people knew best to get out of his way. So she'd managed to get her nemesis off the ground and on the way to a hospital while another guest had enough sense to call his parents to let them know what had happened.

She breathed a sigh of relief.

"Thank you."

Maya jumped when The Old Woman, Lena, appeared by her side. Even in heels it annoyed her that she had to look up at a teenager. The kid was nearly a foot taller than she was in spite of Maya having braided her hair high in a bun on the top her head. But Lena looked shaken. Maya awkwardly wrapped an arm around her waist. "He's going to be okay."

Lena wiped her tears. "He'd better be otherwise you'll be charged with murder."

"He's not going to die."

"Not from lack of trying."

Maya removed her arm. Traitor. "Not you too."

"Everyone knows how much you hate him."

"Not enough to face a prison sentence." Besides she'd done the math more than once and he wasn't worth even the cost of involuntary manslaughter. Cool, sustaining hatred was enough.

"I know," Lena said with a small smile. "I just wanted to say it." She sent Maya a considering look before she said, "It's a shame you hate each other so much."

She walked away, remaining the enigma Maya thought she was. She was too young to know their history, too naïve to understand the depths of contempt.

Their mutual hatred wasn't a shame. It was a way of life.

4

———

SHE PROBABLY SHOULD HAVE SKIPPED the reception. She'd wanted to but encouraging texts from her mother such as:

You'd better make an appearance or your grandmother will haunt you.

You'd better be here soon or I'll find you.

And

You must be there for you sisters. Try to be a good example. I'll tolerate you being a shame to us but not a disappointment.

Gave Maya little choice but to arrive at the lively ballroom where people were dancing and drinking with abandon. There were enough people enjoying themselves at the reception to make the bouquet tossing disaster briefly leave her thoughts.

Fortunately, there were enough people who hadn't been at the wedding ceremony so her humiliating event was not widely known—yet.

Maya took a small plate of canapés from one of the waiters and was about to take a bite when a lethal-looking leopard dressed in a fire engine red gown (one of the three outfits her sister would change into throughout the evening) pounced, baring her teeth.

She snatched the plate from Maya. "What are you doing here?"

Maya popped the canapé in her mouth. She held up her forefinger, hoping for her sister's patience. It was rude to talk with one's mouth full.

Her sister pinched her lips so tight she looked as if she'd sucked a lemon and fastened her mouth with super glue.

Maya, used to her sister's temper, calmly swallowed before she said, "Why am I here?"

"Yes," Gwen barely managed to say.

"Why wouldn't I be?"

"Because you ruined everything," she said, her words briefly drowned out by the laughter of the crowd and the booming voice of the DJ.

Maya gestured to the crowd. "If this is ruined, sign me up." She grabbed a champagne glass.

Gwen snatched it from her. "How could you do this to me?"

Her sister could be dramatic and selfish considering she wasn't the one who'd had to be taken to the hospital.

"You act as if you don't even care."

Maya sighed, eying the champagne glass in longing. "About you or about him?"

"Is everything a joke to you?"

"No, your day isn't over yet and he's going to be fine."

"My wedding day would have been perfect if not for you."

"It would have been perfect if you hadn't tossed the bouquet at me."

Gwen gasped, resting a hand on her chest. "You're blaming me for this?"

"Not entirely—"

A large hand rested on Gwen's shoulder. Maya looked up and saw her new brother-in-law. He'd also changed into a red kaftan and they looked like a matching set. "At least apologize," he said.

Maya shot him a glance in no mood for a scolding. He meant well and was trying his best to appease his new wife, but Maya wasn't ready to help him practice what would have to become a lifelong skill. "Stay out of it. We're family now. I don't have to be nice if I don't want to. And right now I don't want to." She rested a hand on her chest. "No offense."

"No offense taken," he said before he took the precariously held champagne glass from his wife's hand and wisely turned on his shiny black heel and left.

"Now you're insulting my husband?"

Maya gestured to him smiling with one of the guests. "Does he look insulted?"

Gwen pinched the bridge of her nose. "I can't believe you did this."

"Relax, no one here even knows what happened."

"Some do."

"Not enough."

"You shouldn't be here."

Maya began to reply before she spotted the other leopard eying her, the female leopard's bright red lipstick unmistakable as well as the leonine gaze she shared with her daughter. "Blame Mom. She said—"

"I don't care. I don't want you here."

"Oh, you don't mean that," Maya said used to her sister's exaggeration, especially if Maya inadvertently took attention from her. She'd say things like: I wish you'd never moved in with us (when Maya got an A on a test and Gwen a B plus). I wish you'd never been born (when Maya had gotten notice of a scholarship on Gwen's birthday). Minor things like that.

"I do mean it," Gwen said. "Every word. People are talking about you instead of me. This was supposed to be *my* day."

"It still is. You look gorgeous by the way."

"Shut up," Gwen said unable to hide her pleasure. The moment quickly passed. "You ruined my wedding."

"You've said that already. Saying it twice doesn't make it true."

"It is true."

"If I'd stood up and said I was pregnant with the groom's child or that he had a secret family in Nevada then that would have ruined your wedding, but the ceremony was perfect."

"Until you destroyed everything."

Maya inwardly groaned. Her sister was determined not to forgive her. She was not going to get over it and let it pass. So there was no point in arguing. "I did warn you."

Gwen's brows shot up. "And this is how you get back at me?"

"It was an accident, truly." My goodness, did she really look dangerous enough to kill? Why wouldn't anyone believe that she hadn't done it on purpose? If she'd wanted to hurt Keeden she would have found a slower less public way.

Gwen motioned to the exit, the large diamond on her hand catching the light. "Go home. I don't want to see you. I don't want anyone to see you. I don't want you in any pictures. I want you gone."

Maya glanced at the mother leopard. "But Mom—"

"I'll take care of Mom."

"Okay."

"I'll never forgive you."

"Fine," Maya said unfazed, but annoyed and hungry. "I guess I'll just take back the ten-piece essential cookware set I bought you."

Her sister's eyes lit with greedy desire. Maya knew how much she wanted it.

"Did you really get it? You'd better not be lying."

"I'm not lying."

"How could you afford it without a job?"

"My side hustle as a Nigerian prince has been lucrative."

"No need to be a smartass."

"Then don't insult me." Maya took a step forward towards the gift table. "Of course if you hate me so much and will never forgive me, there's no reason to give you my clearly imaginary gift."

Gwen grabbed her arm, stopping her. "Leave it," she said with thinning patience. "I'll forgive you tomorrow."

"Such generosity. Thank you."

"Go."

"Can I at least get something to eat?"

"No."

Maya held up her thumb and forefinger. "Not even something really small like a—?"

"Go Maya."

She shrugged. "Okay. Enjoy the rest of the evening."

"I will once you're gone."

5

———————

Maya let the soothing voice of the older woman on her cell phone screen sweep away her anxieties, the only bright image in her darkened room.

She leaned back against her headboard and listened to the soft sound of a makeup brush gently sweep against the microphone.

"You've been taking good care of your skin."

At one time called whisper videos, the subculture of autonomous sensory meridian response (ASMR) videos was where Maya felt she belonged. In this world there was a mother like figure who told her she looked nice. Who did her hair and told her she was proud of her. A world where she wasn't blamed for every unfortunate event.

Unlike other groups on the internet the ASMR world wasn't infested with trolls but people, whether creators or comments, who wanted and were eager to support each other. Most people thought it was sexual, but only a small fraction of listeners and creators were focused on that sector. Instead the art form created a safe haven.

And she desperately needed one.

Most times she used the videos to help her unwind, sometimes they helped her to fall asleep. She liked the soothing voice, the soft sound of a comb brushing through hair, even nails lightly tapping against a coffee mug.

Here she felt safe.

Here she wasn't constantly reminded that she'd failed so many dreams, that she was a disappointment.

"Here, let me put some eyeliner on."

Only a year ago, she'd thought her life was in order. But then the small liberal arts college where she'd been hired as an art professor lost funding and despite a wide search she hadn't managed to find another job.

Then nine months ago she'd been forced, due to financial necessity, to leave her lovely Pennsylvania town and move back to the family house in Maryland when her landlord raised the rent of her townhouse by fifty percent (because he could).

"Let me do your hair."

Maya blinked back tears. As much as she pretended it didn't hurt, it did. It hurt to be the butt of jokes, to be so different than everyone else even when she wasn't trying. Just like her flower hatred, few cared about how much she'd loved being a professor and what a loss it had been to her.

Art didn't register in her household—except when it came to Keeden. He was a true artist: A rich, globe-trotting, world renowned artist.

But she didn't want to think about him. She didn't want to have nightmares.

The day had been nightmarish enough.

She'd returned home from the reception, changed into leggings and a large T-shirt, heated up leftovers (jollof rice and chicken), then called one of the doctors and learned there wasn't much more to report about Keeden's condition.

He was still breathing and that was enough for her.

She finished the video then set the cell phone down, the glow of the screen illuminating the side table where a book about finance sat. She might have to retrain and gain new skills if she didn't find employment soon. As much as the thought galled her.

She didn't remember falling asleep. But she must have because she woke up the next morning to someone moving her back and forth like a rolling pin.

"How can you sleep when a man's life hangs in the balance?"

Maya slowly became more awake and quickly discovered that "someone" was her mother. No surprise there. She'd rather be treated like a rolling pin than hit with one.

She rubbed her eyes. "He's not going to die. I checked."

"Get up, shower and change and then we'll go."

"Go where?"

Her mother left the room and closed the door in response.

Two hours later Maya found herself having a mild panic attack.

She stood in the center of the flower shop trying to make her heart stop racing, hoping that nobody noticed the beads of sweat on her forehead or that she couldn't manage to stop her left hand from twitching.

She was in this awful place because of her mother.

Maya had been an unwitting victim to her mother's diabolical plan. She'd let her mother bully her into her mother's prized Lexus by telling Maya how she hadn't been able to sleep and telling her that she needed help running errands and since Maya had nothing better to do, she had to come along.

Maya should have known her mother had other designs

when she locked the doors, snaring Maya in her carefully laid trap.

But she hadn't suspected a thing.

She still hadn't suspected much until they slowed at a stop-light and her mother had dropped the bombshell. "You're going to send him flowers."

Maya turned sharply to her. "I'm going to send who what?"

"You heard me." The light turned green. She put her foot on the gas.

Maya resisted the urge to pound the window, gripped by the same fear of someone being kidnapped. She tried to lower the window. It didn't budge. There was no way to jump out of the moving car.

She took a deep breath, trying to tap down her rising panic. She would keep her voice rational. "Why would I send flowers? Why not a fruit basket or–"

"Flowers."

"Okay, fine. I'll send him flowers. I'll order them online."

"It's not the same."

"Of course it's not the same! That's the entire point."

"You will go to the flower shop, select something then you will have them delivered."

"Why don't you order something and I'll pay—"

"No, it must come from you. You have to put in the effort."

"Can't we just lie and say that I did all that you wanted me to do?"

"Did I raise a liar?"

Maya sighed and closed her eyes. No amount of argument could dissuade her mother.

That's how Maya found herself alone in the last place she wanted to be. She was alone because the moment they'd entered the shop, her mother's cell phone had rung and she said, "Order something showy and expensive," before dashing out of the store.

Flowers surrounded her, enveloping her in their scent. Each one mocking her. *What right do you have to be in here? You couldn't tell a peony from a tulip, an African violet from a blooming cactus.*

Did she really have to send the one thing she hated to the one person she hated more?

"Can I help you?"

Maya turned to the kindly assistant, shoving her twitching left hand into the pocket of her jacket.

"Do you have anything for a funeral?" She hadn't meant to say that although that's how she felt, as if she were preparing for her own demise. "I'm kidding. It's sort of a funeral, the death of my pride, dignity, but never mind." She was babbling because she was nervous and wanted to be anywhere else but there. The sight of the flowers made her feel dizzy and queasy. She didn't even remember exactly what she'd said (something about someone being hit by a car, needing something demure but cheery and expensive enough to show off) only that she'd made the clerk smile and that was a win since few people seemed to like her recently.

She gave the address where the flowers should be delivered then hurried out of the store, wiping sweat from her forehead. She'd made it. It was over.

She'd survived.

Her mother was still on the phone. Even though she was in the car, she spoke loud enough for Maya to hear her through the windscreen, as well as the person on the other end of the conversation since her mother apparently had them on speaker-phone. She motioned Maya to get in the car. But a conversation in surround sound was the last thing she needed.

Maya pretended not to see her and turned her back and

looked at the storefront. She'd wait outside the car until her mother finished her conversation.

Finally she heard the car door open. "How much did you spend?"

Maya got in the car and put on her seatbelt. "Enough."

"Will it show?"

"Yes. I instructed the attendant to put the price tag on the bottom of the vase."

Her mother whacked her. "Why must you be so cheeky?"

Maya rubbed her shoulder. "I don't know. Part of my charm, I guess."

"I asked you a serious question and I expect a serious response. Look at me."

Maya sighed and faced her mother. "They won't be able to miss how truly sorry I am."

Her mother searched her face as if trying to catch her in a lie then nodded, satisfied. "Good."

It should have been the end of it. She'd done everything her mother had wanted.

But two days later she walked into the kitchen and spotted her parents sitting at the kitchen table. They looked at her with an icy, cold blast of silence.

Her stepfather mumbled something to her mother before he stood, sent her another cryptically cold glance then left the room.

Her mother kept her head bent.

"What's going on?" Maya asked.

"You must apologize."

"To whom?"

"Adesina."

"But I've already apologized. I sent flowers, remember?"

She glared at her. "You will go and apologize in person."

She pointed at her. "You must undo the damage you have done."

"What have I done now?"

"I think you already know."

"I honestly don't. Even if I did, do I have to apologize in person? Can't we video chat?"

"You will see him or may the wrath of God wipe you from the face of the earth." She stormed out of the kitchen.

Her sister Ava entered the kitchen looking worried. "Mom looks furious. What have you done now?"

Maya collapsed into a chair. "I honestly wish I knew."

6

____

The snake was sunning on his favorite rock.

The Adesina family home boasted a sunroom with a chaise lounge that Keeden preferred. Although he had his own house, one Maya'd never seen and had no interest in doing so, not much caring to see whatever cave he slithered out from when he was in his true form, he'd chosen to stay in the family home to recuperate.

She didn't like being alone with him, but she'd separated from her mother in the foyer and found her way to his favorite spot eager to quickly apologize for whatever new slight she'd done and then leave.

She walked into the light bathed sunroom and noticed he was wearing a black and white batakan, or Ghanaian smock, and jeans which was rare since he usually didn't wear traditional African clothing. She took a seat facing him, "Thank Ghana it's Friday."

His face turned to thunder. "Come to finish the job?"

Maya crossed her legs and swung her foot. "You're gorgeous when you're angry." Which was a lie since she couldn't stand to look at him. But another woman might find smooth cocoa skin stretched over high cheekbones, thick, ink black hair that glistened in the sunlight worn in two long braids, and full pillow soft lips—or so she'd heard them described—attractive.

"You tried to kill me."

The one thing that disturbed her the most about him was his voice. He had a rich, deep voice that was ill-suited to his thin frame. And as much as she hated him she always had to steel herself from the effects of it because it was like melted butter on a warm croissant.

She looked at her nails gaining the courage to face him again. "If I'd tried to kill you, you'd be lying in a coffin not on a lounge chair," she said meeting his eyes.

He lifted his arm, wrapped in a cast. "I might as well be dead. Do you know what you've cost me?"

"You'll heal."

He mumbled something she couldn't hear. "What?"

"On top of a fractured wrist, a concussion, a twisted ankle," he continued.

"But no broken ribs, your spine's intact." She clasped her hands together and smiled. "Look at the bright side."

He sent her a dark look. "What's the bright side?"

"Considering how skinny you are, I'm actually surprised you didn't snap in two like a twig."

He hadn't put on an ounce of fat in more than twenty years. He'd grown taller but still reminded her of the lanky sixteen-year-old she'd first met at fourteen. She'd foolishly thought they might be friends, and at the time she had thought he was cute in a vampiric sort of way. Even back then he'd mainly worn black and she'd initially thought he wore eyeliner until she learned his eyelashes were so naturally thick that he looked like he was wearing makeup.

She'd pegged him as another outsider, like her. His mother had been Ghanaian who'd given him his first name and had passed away when he was ten, his father had soon remarried and they had a daughter who was their pride and joy. Plus she'd seen some of his artwork—he'd won two national contests—and had been impressed.

She'd enthusiastically told him so and he'd dismissed her with a superior look of disdain. Used to being rebuffed, she tried to get to know him on several other occasions and at one point he had seemed to like her too, or at least tolerated her, but she'd been wrong. He'd eventually shown that he'd thought she was beneath him.

At first she'd been disappointed. Her disdain for him had been a slow build. There'd be a small slight here, another there before they began to add up.

The Adesinas had lived in New York at the time, they'd moved to Maryland seven years ago, so she didn't see him often. Perhaps four times a year at special events, which was more than enough. She'd had to endure his haughty glances, his cruel smiles and biting words. But she'd taken it all in stride.

She disliked him, but she hadn't hated him.

Until.

Until one day, ten years ago, at the spring party of a mutual family friend. He'd made one casual, contemptuously cruel comment that had not only shamed her in front of everyone, shattering the fragile, yet carefully built reputation she'd tried to hold on to, but had also frozen her heart against him forever.

She'd learned to hate him that day. Hating him felt better than being hurt.

Because he'd definitely hurt her. And she refused to give him that kind of power.

"You mean disappointed."

"What?" Maya said clearing her thoughts. Oh, the snake

was still talking.

"You're disappointed I didn't snap it two, not surprised."

She uncrossed her legs and leaned forward. "It's still on my bucket list."

"I never realized how much you hated me."

"My hatred for you keeps me warm on winter nights."

"Then yours pales in comparison. Mine would incinerate."

She shrugged unconcerned. "You've always been an over-achiever."

He briefly closed his eyes as if in pain. "You want to destroy me."

"That's a little dramatic."

Keeden glared at her. "Dramatic? Do you know the incalculable damage you've done?"

"I am sorry."

Her apology didn't appease him. He narrowed his eyes and lowered his voice. "Too bad you miscalculated."

Maya shook her head. The banter had changed. There was a cool calculating gleam in his eyes she found unsettling. She stood. She'd apologized and now it was time to go. "I would never miscalculate your demise."

"Mathematics aren't your strong suit."

She'd failed calculus—dashing any parental hopes that she'd become a doctor, not that she wanted to be, but that was beside the point. Keeden knew her weakness and would never let her forget it.

"How many fingers am I holding up?" she said flashing two vulgar V signs.

"I gave you too much credit. I thought you were more mature than this. Did you think your little joke was amusing?"

"Joke?"

Before he had a chance to reply, a scream pierced through the air.

MAYA SPUN TO THE ENTRYWAY, startled. "What on earth?"

"I guess your mother didn't find it funny either," Keeden said in an ironic tone.

"Find what funny?"

"Come on, Maya. Don't act innocent. It doesn't suit you."

"I honestly don't know what you're talking about."

His penetrating dark eyes softened a fraction, uncertain, which was a little unnerving because he'd never looked at her like that before. However, he didn't get a chance to say anything. Her mother appeared in the doorway, grasping her chest and breathing hard.

"Mom," Maya said alarmed.

Her mother rushed forward and Maya opened her arms in case her mother was about to collapse, although she feared she wasn't strong enough to catch her. Instead her mother stopped a yard away from her and whacked Maya on the side of the head. "You shameless girl!"

Maya silently swore. She bit her lip trying not to imagine the smug grin likely on Keeden's face. She knew he took perverse pleasure in seeing her humiliated. She threw her hands in the air, exasperated. "Please, tell me what's going on? What did I do?"

Mrs. Adesina, Keeden's stepmother, an elegant figure in a purple colored pant suit, came into the room holding a large bouquet. Her mother pointed at it like a prosecutor pointing out the evidence of a crime. "What do you call this?"

Dear God what was she expected to say? "Um...Flowers?"

She hit her again. "Don't be daft."

"Clearly I am because I don't know what you want me to say."

Mrs. Adesina looked near tears. "So distasteful." She set the vase down on the circular wooden table. "How could you?"

Maya turned to her mother. "You asked me to send flowers."

"Yes, but not for a funeral."

"A funeral?" She took a shaky step forward and studied the bouquet. She had vaguely wondered why all the blossoms were white.

White like flowers at a gravesite.

Oh dear God it was a funeral bouquet.

Her skin felt clammy, the flowers began to sway from an unknown breeze. Suddenly she was swept back to the memory of her grandmother's funeral. There had been huge wreaths of white ribbons, white blossoms among lush greens. She remembered overhearing a guest saying they'd gotten a heartfelt condolences arrangement—white roses and pompons to convey sympathy and comfort during grief. Another guest had complimented the various bouquets saying they gave a sense of peaceful heavenly hope.

But the sight of them had given Maya no peace. They stole it from her. Then as much as now. Her heart pounded so hard it hurt. She stumbled back and sat down hard on the seat.

Damn flowers. They'd betrayed her again. Mocked her. Shamed her. Why couldn't flowers just be flowers? Why did there have to be a hidden message?

She looked at Keeden and opened her mouth, but no words emerged.

Partially from shock but partially from the way he was looking back at her. As if he was worried. The last thing she'd want was this man's concern.

She cleared her throat and looked at Mrs. Adesina. "I didn't send those," her voice sounded hoarse but at least it was audible.

Mrs. Adesina read the card. "With sympathy, Maya."

She waved her hands, released a bitter laugh. "No, no the clerk got it wrong. They didn't realize I was kidding."

"So you did think this was a joke?"

"No, not at all. You know I hate flowers and I hate—" She looked at the snake and held her tongue. "There's been a misunderstanding. I—"

A whack on the back of the head stopped the rest of her words. "Stop making excuses."

"I'm not," Maya said annoyed her voice had risen to a whine, but her mother's whacks hurt. She was certain her mother carried rocks in her purse.

"You pushed him in front of a car," her mother said.

"I didn't push him intentionally. I knocked into him by accident. Why is everyone accusing me of something that was an accident? Do I look homicidal?" She pointed at him. "You are not allowed to answer that."

Her mother pushed past her and went to Keeden's side. "Are you in much pain?"

He squeezed his eyes shut. "Agony, Aunty," he said addressing her with respect. "Every time I close my eyes I get

flashbacks," his silky voice almost made his words sound inde-
cent. No wonder her mother was so easily seduced.

"Poor, dear boy."

He opened his eyes and fixed Maya with a cool stare. "But
I'll manage."

She met his gaze, relieved that his look of concern had
vanished. This was the man she loved to hate. She was sorry
he'd gotten hurt, but she refused to be riddled with guilt.

"I need to rest now, Aunty," he said.

Maya gritted her teeth annoyed by how he kept using the
reverential address.

"Of course. Of course." Her mother nodded, solemn. "We
will make this up to you."

"It's not funny."

Maya glared at her two sisters who couldn't stop laughing
as they sat in the café booth their iced coffee and chocolate
muffins left half eaten. She'd needed to get out of the house and
Ava had decided to treat them, but Maya hadn't managed to eat
a thing.

"You sent him funeral flowers?" Ava said.

"With a note?" Cat added, wiping her eyes.

Maya sighed, used to being a source of amusement. They
were both taller than she was which had been annoying as a
teenager when people thought she was the youngest although
she was the eldest. They had better temperaments. They
managed to please their parents in ways Maya never could. Ava
because she was a natural people pleaser with a sweet face to
match and Catherine (Cat for short) because she looked so
plain and fragile people feared a harsh word would break her.

Her mother never whacked them. However, unlike Gwen,

Maya liked them and to her surprise, they liked her, so she didn't mind them having a giggle at her expense. "It was all a mistake." She folded her arms, trying to look fierce but failing. "Really."

Ava shook her head. "We knew you hated the guy."

Cat nodded. "But this was extreme."

"Mom will never forgive you."

"And Aunty Florence."

"And the Tosins."

"Oh yes, he's their godson, isn't he?"

Ava and Cat looked at each other then burst into new peals of laughter.

"Calm down," Maya said, looking around the crowded café at the people looking at them. "Or they'll throw us out."

They sobered.

"You really did it this time," Ava said.

Cat picked up her muffin. Her second (not that Maya was counting, although it galled her that her sister could out eat her and still look emaciated). "You've caused a family crisis."

Maya shook her head and waved her hand unfazed. "It'll blow over. I doubt it's that bad."

8

———

It was that bad.

A day later Maya sat in the family living room, facing a semi-circle of her parents and four other elders.

She'd been summoned.

It would have been a scary, solemn affair if her mother hadn't left a Nollywood comedy on the 72 inch flat screen on the wall. It was on mute but still...

Maya clasped her hands determined not to smile at the antics on the screen. Instead she tried to focus on the people in the room.

Her parents looked ready to disown her. No surprise there. What did surprise her were the other people in the room. People like Uncle Martin and their former pastor.

Why was their former pastor there? The one whose sermons usually made Maya doze off? True, the pastor's sermons were in Yoruba, which Maya was terrible at, and long (Maya was also terrible at keeping attention for too long) but she didn't have that much sway anymore, did she?

The pastor sat like an ostrich—long neck and round body

with a beak of a nose. But what was she doing there? Her parents went to an English church now. Either it was an intervention or a family meeting of the elders. Not a good sign.

"The Kayodes and Adesinas have been united," the head elder said, a bearlike man with a thin mustache, whose deep voice could fill an auditorium without the use of a microphone. "Will always be united."

Yes through wind, through storms, through fire, through wars the Adesinas had been there. She'd heard the tales since childhood. They'd sounded interesting the first hundred times then somewhere around a thousand they just lost their lovely patina.

"A bond nothing can break," the elder continued.

Dear God why couldn't she remember his name? Papa something. If only she could remember who his eldest child was. Wait he'd been widowed, right?

She felt a pinch. "Are you listening?" her mother hissed.

Not a jot. "Yes, of course."

"We have known the Adesinas for centuries," the elder continued.

"Yeah," Maya said, hoping to lighten the mood. "Don't you think that's long enough?"

Her mother's frown increased. "This is serious."

"I'm being serious."

"Excuse our daughter's flippancy. I did not raise her well."

Maya hated when her mother did that. Anytime Maya failed at something she would guilt trip her by saying what a terrible mother she was. At times Maya wanted to remind her that she hadn't raised her for nine years and maybe that was to blame. But she never wanted to shame her grandmother's name. Any mistake or flaw was hers and no one else's.

Maya pressed her hands together, briefly bowing her head,

looking demure wasn't her strong suit but she'd try. "I don't mean to be rude, but can we get to the point?"

"You have shamed all of us," the pastor said.

"And you must fix it," another elder said, a woman dressed in an expensive blue suit that looked a size too small. Maya half feared if the elder breathed too deep one of the silver buttons would pop off and take out someone's eye.

"I've apologized."

The elder pointed at her. "You sent flowers meant for a funeral."

Maya shifted to the side, seeing the fabric dangerously stretch against the buttons, ready to dodge any unexpected projectiles. "I told you I should have sent a fruit basket." She held up her hands at the look of outrage on her mother's face. "And I apologized for the flower mix-up too."

Martin cleared his throat. "This must be remedied by more than token actions."

Maya grinned. "Aw...look at you trying to sound smart." Martin had only managed to be part of the elders by an accident of birth. Her paternal grandfather had gotten randy at eighty and had another son, making him her uncle even though he was seven years her junior. But he was an irritant, a delightful one. She saw his lips pinch, but the pastor covered his hand.

"This will take more than that," she said.

"Such as?"

"He's an artist..."

Maya shifted in her seat and stared at the TV, wishing she could laugh but feeling like crying instead. She didn't need to be reminded of the great and wonderful Keeden Adesina whose work has been seen across the globe.

"...He has injured his wrist and has a major project coming up. You will assist him."

Assist him? Help that smug, arrogant, skinny little prick with anything? Absolutely never.

Would *Oh hell no* be the right answer? Probably not. Hysterical laughter maybe. No, that wouldn't be appropriate either. Maya cleared her throat. Clearly they were joking.

"You don't have anything to say?" the head elder said.

She drummed her fingers on her knees. "I'm waiting for the punchline."

"There is no punchline. You're going to work for him until his cast comes off."

"I'd rather cut out my tongue."

Her mother sent her a dark look. "Don't give me ideas."

"But—"

"You're unemployed."

The words stung. It wasn't as if she was unemployed on purpose. They treated it like a personal failing instead of a misfortune. "I'm looking."

"It's been months. Martin's nephew only took two weeks."

"He's an aesthetician."

"If you'd been one too, finding work wouldn't have been hard."

She wasn't going to have this circular argument again. "I will find a proper job. I have bills to pay." She lowered her voice, "I even pay you rent—"

"You won't have to worry about that anymore," her stepfather said.

"What? Why?"

"You'll be moving out."

9

———

Her ears started ringing.

"It'll be for the best," Martin said in a self-satisfied voice.

Maya leaned forward certain she'd misheard. "Did you say move out?"

"Yes," her mother said.

Her stepfather clasped his hands together. "Fortunately, he has plenty of room to accommodate you."

Maya looked around the room, her skin feeling clammy and sticky. Why were they looking at her as if this was a clever idea? What kind of ludicrous...

"Accommodate me?"

"Yes, so you won't be in each other's way," he explained as if she didn't know what the word meant.

Maya surged to her feet. "You're kicking me out of the family house?"

Her stepfather nodded. "It's a perfect solution."

"No, it's not!"

Her mother gestured to the chair. "Sit down."

"If you do this to me I'll sing a song of curses that will last a day."

"And if you don't do this," her mother countered. "I'll sing a song of curses that will last a year."

She believed her. Her mother could be imaginative. She fell back into her chair in defeat.

"It won't be forever," her stepfather said.

"But we must heal ties between the families," the second elder said.

Maya rubbed the back of her neck. "D-did he agree to this?"

They fell silent.

Her heart lifted with hope. If she were in a musical she'd burst into song. "He doesn't know." She clasped her hands together. "Praise God."

Her mother pointed a warning finger at her. "Don't be flippant."

She was saved. There was *no way* Keeden would want her living under his roof, even in servitude. She had to resist the urge to sing Louis Armstrong's version of "What a Wonderful World."

"Do you agree?" Papa-something said.

"There's nothing to agree to," Maya said, trying her best not to smile. "He won't—"

"He will."

But he won't. Never. Ever. But she'd placate them. "If he agrees, then I'll agree."

"Good."

But Maya knew he wouldn't.

Not in a million years.

∾

"Think about it as an opportunity. You wouldn't have to worry about food or rent and your parents wouldn't bother you about getting a job because you have one. There are a lot of upsides."

Maya paced her bedroom trying to let the advice of her former colleague and friend pierce the looming feeling of dread that hung over her head.

Doris still lived in Pennsylvania and had decided to retire rather than seek new employment. Maya envied her friend's choice since her job search was leading nowhere. Doris was one of the few friends who had time to talk to her. Priya always had someone else's screaming baby somewhere in the background because she couldn't say no and Lars was so obsessed with achieving tenure he could talk of nothing else.

"Right," Maya said with false cheer. "An opportunity. All I have to do is work for and live with a man whose glance could turn hell into the Arctic."

"You could always move in with me. I have the space."

She did. Doris owned a lovely craftsman style home that she'd gotten after her divorce. But she also had a forty-year-old son who refused to move out after a "recent" divorce that had happened seven years ago. Maya had met him on three occasions (Doris's poor attempts at trying to match them up) and found him as sexually appealing as a termite infested tree stump.

She'd rather live with her parents.

But now even that option had been taken from her.

"Thanks, but I'll be fine. I'm venting because I'm insulted but I'm not really worried because he'll say no and then that will be the end of it." She stopped pacing and stared out her window, watching a dog walker manage three Russell Terriers that all seemed to want to go in different directions. "Unless he wanted to be spiteful." She could picture him grinning with malicious glee at the thought of having her at his beck and call.

She couldn't allow for that possibility. She had to go to Keeden and make sure the thought didn't cross his mind.

Or if it did, she'd make sure he'd think it was the worst idea in the world.

10

————

Naturally she found the snake in the garden.

Maya had barely managed to convince Mrs. Adesina to let her speak to Keeden and had expected to be led to the sunroom, but instead she'd walked pass it to the garden out back and motioned Maya forward, warning her not to stay too long.

Maya gripped her hands into fists, knowing, for the sake of appearances, she had to move forward into a landscape bursting with flowers, but found it a struggle.

Mrs. Adesina tilted her head concerned. "Are you okay?"

No, not really. "I'm fine," Maya said, plastering on a smile before she marched ahead like a soldier off to battle. She walked a few yards before she turned and saw that she was no longer being watched. Mrs. Adesina had gone.

She was on her own.

She turned back to her target. She saw him standing in the gazebo surrounded by climbing vines and an array of roses. She hesitated. Damn, why did there have to be flowers every-where? She rubbed her nose against their invading fragrance;

the sun's rays illuminated the petals' radiance, making Keeden's silhouette appear even darker and more dangerous in comparison. He stood with his back to her. He was of average height, but was taller than her and his superior and imposing stance always made her feel shorter than she actually was.

She didn't want to talk to him here.

She could always come back later, talk to him another time. On the phone. Or by text. She could try to persuade him that way.

She bit her lip and carefully took a step back.

"Retreating already?" he said without turning.

She froze. A blue tinged butterfly fluttered past her face.

"It's not like you to back down from a fight."

Leaving now would be cowardice. Maya took a deep breath and walked forward. "I didn't come here to fight."

"So you've heard," Keeden said taking a seat.

Maya stepped into the gazebo, wishing her hands didn't feel suddenly damp. "Yes."

"And you want to beg me to disagree with them."

Yes. "No." She swallowed. "I know you already do."

"Really?"

"Yes. I came here because I wanted to reject this ridiculous plan as a united front because I know you think this is an awful idea as much as I do."

He lifted a brow. "Go on."

He was listening. That was a good sign. "I think it's very disrespectful that they'd choose me to help you with your work. Something very important to you. I'm sure you can find a more suitable assistant. I'd help you if that would appease them, but you wouldn't want to see me every day, have me under foot every day. Going through your things."

He blinked but didn't reply.

"Although I'm sure you'd considered this as a great opportunity for revenge."

"I'm still tempted."

"But you wouldn't want to risk your reputation."

His brows shot up. "You'd sabotage my work?"

"No...I'd do my best but you're used to people of a different caliber and I'm not even close." Stroking his ego made her stomach churn but she was desperate.

He nodded.

She sighed relieved. "I'm so glad we both agree it's a terrible idea. Why anyone would think I should help you with your work is beyond absurd."

"Is it really?" a familiar deep voice said.

Maya's heart started to race. She stared at the ground then her sneakers then the ground again. She knew the owner of the voice and he always made her tongue tied. Thank goodness he hadn't been at the wedding.

"Stay out of this," Keeden said.

The continued sound of his approaching footsteps up the gazebo steps made it clear the man planned to ignore the warning. "I heard what the elders had planned and I think it could work. Why wouldn't you help him?"

A yellow rose came into view.

Maya slowly lifted her head and gazed at the tall, dark skinned man with a smile as white and sweet as a marshmallow. Bryant Meadows, the son of a Nigerian mother and black British father, was a wonderful and smart man who had great taste in all things that mattered except in who he'd chosen to be close to him. How Bryant could be the cretin's best friend she couldn't fathom.

"She hates flowers," Keeden said.

He abruptly withdrew the flower. "I'm sorry. I forgot."

"I-it's okay," Maya said taking the offered gift, ignoring the thorn that pricked into her finger, causing it to bleed.

She heard Keeden swear. "Give her a tissue or napkin."

"Why?"

"'Cause she's bleeding."

"I-I'm fine," Maya said feeling the sticky trail of blood slide down her wrist. She sucked on her finger then held up her finger when the bleeding stopped. "See?"

"But it's still on your arm."

"It will dry," she said through gritted teeth. Bryant had given her a gift. She'd endure whatever pain to keep this moment special. She liked to please him.

He took a seat next to Keeden, his warm brown eyes fixed on hers, the faintest hint of the British accent he'd acquired before leaving England at thirteen, touching his words when he said, "You're sure you're okay?"

Maya nodded and lifted the rose to her nose and pretended to inhale it as if she enjoyed its lovely scent, resisting the urge to snap the head off and toss it, and the stem, on the ground and wipe her hands afterwards. She plastered on another smile and set the rose on the bench beside her. "T-thank you."

He shook his head. "Don't thank me."

She frowned. "Why not?"

"Because he's trying to bribe you," Keeden said.

"That's right," Bryant said, folding his arms, stretching the material of his yellow T-shirt across his broad chest. "I think the elders have come up with a great idea."

When he was around her body felt limp, her mouth refused to work. Her brain too. It went completely blank.

He'd spoken to her. But somehow she couldn't fashion a reply.

Such blazing beauty. Such warmth. How could she disagree with him? Whenever he was around all feelings of bitterness, anger, annoyance fled and she was left like this. Like a bowl of mush.

"It's not a good idea," Keeden said, his deep voice slapping her out of her paralysis like a cold ocean wave.

He yanked her out of her dream. Like a guitar string snapping, whenever Bryant was around Keeden's voice had all the musical beauty of an out of tune piano.

"He's too proud to admit it," Bryant said. "But we could use the help."

They owned a thriving business together (best friends and business partners, Maya still couldn't fathom how Bryant managed it) that licensed and published their works. Bryant was a graphic artist and writer who'd collaborated with Keeden on a number of projects including art prints, textiles, illustrated books and the like.

"No, we don't," Keeden said.

"We?" Maya said.

Bryant nodded. "Yeah, I'm crashing at his place for awhile due to some renovations at mine."

What!!! If she were a firework, she'd shoot into the sky and burst into a million little flames. He was staying at Keeden's house? She'd get to see him every day? She'd get to be close to him? She'd get a chance to overcome her shyness and maybe, just maybe, ask him out?

Keeden shook his head. "We've agreed. She's not—"

"I'll do it."

Keeden stared at her open mouthed, but Bryant's smile was the only thing that mattered. He showered her in a brilliant light of white. "Great."

His cell phone rang. "Excuse me." He stood and left.

And it was as if the sun disappeared and she was left with darkness.

Darkness spoke first. "You're pathetic."

She felt like a rocket that had crashed back to earth. "Shut up."

"You—"

"I know that I have a slim chance with him and I don't care. I really don't care. I don't care that everyone laughs at me behind my back and that he probably finds me a blithering idiot." She paused. "No, I want to change that and here's my chance."

"You're using this for your own purposes."

Maya shrugged. "Yeah, why not?"

"What do I get out of this?"

"I won't torture you."

"Really?"

"Yes."

Keeden stared at her for a long moment before he said, "Explain to me how the sight of you every day *in my home* won't be torture."

Damn, he had a point. But she had to make this work even if it meant charming a snake.

Maya pressed her hands together. "Here's the deal. I'll make your life better and you help me win over Bryant."

Keeden shook his head. "My life is better without you in it."

She took a deep breath. "I can still improve it."

He glanced at the rose on the bench then met her gaze in a silent challenge as if he wanted to see how desperate she really was. "I'm still not seeing how this will benefit me."

She held his gaze. "On top of helping you with your work, I'll also clean."

"I pay a housekeeper for that."

"I'll cook."

"Something you'd expect me to eat? Never. Besides, I have

a chef for that too. Or Bryant." His eyes brightened with soft mockery. "You know he likes to cook."

Yes, everyone knew how Bryant liked to cook. One day she hoped to eat one of his meals. Her mouth watered just at the thought. Perhaps one night she could convince him to make her a late night snack...

"I'll help you organize your work," Maya said in a rush. "Your gallery showings, your conventions, anything. I'll do it. Give me a month. The sooner you help get Bryant to notice me the sooner I'll be out of your hair."

Keeden sighed. "You're not his type."

"I know. You can help me make a few adjustments. The more you tell me the quicker you get rid of me. Otherwise I'll stick with you until your cast comes off."

He looked away and visibly shudder.

"Eight weeks, right?" Maya said, sensing him waver.

He hung his head and said in surrender, "Okay, two weeks max."

"Four," she countered.

He lifted his gaze and studied her in a way that always made her want to hurl an insult or punch him, but this time she sat still. She could take his disdain. She didn't care if he thought she was pathetic. She was used to him thinking she was lower than dirt.

This was her opportunity to change her life. To be brave and go after the man she loved.

If that meant swallowing Keeden's venom she'd do it. She'd become immune.

"When you used to enter your work in contests," he said, "you occasionally used pastels, right?"

"Yes."

"Do you still have that Sennelier pastel set you bragged about getting?"

"That was years ago." And one of the most expensive treats she'd ever given herself. She'd gotten extra soft pastels of brilliant colors and high quality.

He narrowed his eyes. "Is that a yes or a no?"

"Why?"

He sent a pointed look at her pricked finger. "I think it's a fair trade."

Maya gripped her hand in her lap. She didn't want to part with her wonderful supplies. There were so few things she'd kept before she'd given up being a full time artist or even a part time one. Those pastels tethered her to a dream she might never see come true, but kept her from sinking into sadness. "Why would you need those pastels? You can afford—"

"Do you want my help or not?"

Those wonderful, luxurious pastels (she could still remember how they slid across the paper, how they felt in her hand) represented her past. Exchanging them for Bryant was a chance at a new future. "Okay, I give you the pastels and you give me *three* weeks and tell me everything I need to know."

"Not everything, but I'll tell you enough. The rest is up to you."

Maya jumped to her feet. "Good. It's a deal. I'll see you tomorrow."

She rushed down the gazebo steps, determined not to think about losing her beloved pastels, eager to get out of this horrible garden. She was almost to the patio when she heard him say, "Wait."

She spun around.

He looked a little pale and was breathing too fast as he closed the distance between them. She took a step towards him concerned. "What is it? Have you changed your mind already?"

"No." Keeden held out the yellow rose Bryant had given her. "You left this."

She took an instinctive step back.

Keeden noticed her reaction and flashed a sour grin. "Pretend it's from him not me."

That wasn't it. She wasn't rejecting the flower because he was holding it. Or maybe she was. Maybe the sight of the man she didn't like holding something she found detestable was too much. All she knew was that she didn't want to touch it again. "You can throw it away."

"You don't want his gift?"

"You told me it was a bribe."

He nodded and tossed the flower away. "You're right."

He'd tossed it into a nearby bush where she couldn't see it anymore. She breathed a sigh of relief.

"Clean up your arm when you get inside."

She glanced down and saw she still had a visible stream of dried blood. "No, I think I'll keep it a little longer. Something to remember you by."

He inhaled sharply as if she'd amused him, she noticed his gaze had softened, but then she saw him wince. "Are you okay?"

Any signs of amusement left his face and his tone turned distant. "Relax. You don't have to pretend to care."

He turned and walked back to the gazebo.

"Still a jerk," she muttered as she headed inside. The funny thing was that, for just a tiny moment, she hadn't been pretending.

11

RUNNING after her had been stupid, but at least his ankle had healed.

Keeden eased himself back down on the gazebo bench silently calculating when he could take another dose of pain medicine.

What had possessed him to give her a flower? She hated flowers and he hated her.

And why the hell had he agreed to help the short, evil troll in exchange for a set of pastels?

"Someone looks like they need a hug."

Keeden frowned as Bryant walked up the gazebo steps, a wide smile on his face.

Bryant's smiles always managed to hide how devious he really was.

He flashed one of those deceptive smiles at Keeden as he took a seat.

Keeden wasn't fooled. "I hate you."

Bryant laughed. "No you don't. You're just too proud to admit you need her."

"I need her as much as a venereal disease. An extra ear. A—"

"This deadline is important."

"I know that. But she'll make it worse."

"She's one of the best at woodblock printing that I've seen. A true artist."

Over the years Maya had become an accomplished woodblock artist, although she didn't exhibit professionally. Her work was admired by her students and faculty and, most importantly, by her sisters, Ava and Cat, who showed off their sister's works (likely without Maya's knowledge) online any chance they got. Keeden and Bryant had managed to see her work when Lena sent them links. "Plus she's what we have right now," Bryant continued. "You don't have the luxury to be picky."

Keeden had a large commissioned piece due that should have been done months ago but he'd been procrastinating. Now he had lost two months to finish a project that would take six more months and couldn't because of his cast. He did need help. He just wished it didn't have to be her. "She'll be in my house. In my studio. In my space."

"We'll limit it to certain times. I'll be there, remember? I'll monitor her for you."

Keeden sent him a considering look.

"What?"

"She'd like that."

Bryant furrowed his brows. "She'd like what?"

"You closely monitoring her. Perhaps you could take her out and—"

Bryant shook his head and waved his hands. "No, I'm not stepping into your territory."

"My territory?"

"We both know she's perfect for you."

Keeden knew people could die of shock, but he now wondered if they could die from abject horror. He was certain his heart had briefly stopped. "What?"

"Years of sexual attraction will eventually boil to the surface. Lena gives it another few years, but I think now's the time."

Sexual what? Him with Maya? Attracted to her in anyway? Never. "Have you completely lost your mind? Do you know how much I—"

Bryant nodded like an indulgent uncle dealing with a rambunctious child. "I know. You've told me more than once. She talks too much, she has short legs, she's as thick as clotted cream. I know she's got a bunch of faults but so do you."

"I'm not having this conversation. She's not my type."

"You don't have a type."

"If I did, it wouldn't be a short, stubby gnome of a woman. Besides, she likes you not me."

"When is she moving in?"

Keeden inwardly sighed not surprised Bryant sidestepped the issue. Everyone knew about Maya's giant crush on him, but Bryant continued to play the innocent. Keeden would have to push his friend more if he was going to help Maya with her plan and get her out of his house.

"Tomorrow."

"Good. Best to get started right away and I know you're going stir crazy here. We can leave in an hour. I'll help you prepare for your new assistant."

"I'm not preparing anything," Keeden said in a curt tone. "I have staff for that."

Bryant fell silent then said in a reassuring voice, "You'll get through this. You didn't always hate her."

Keeden rubbed his nose strangely unsettled by his friend's

reminder. Usually he was able to ignore his friend's teasing, but this time he found it harder to shake off.

He'd once briefly—many, many, many years ago—thought she was cute, in a baby bird kind of way. All he could remember was wondering if her mouth ever closed. She never stopped talking.

And she'd talk about anything: The color of the sky, the history of paper, the reason mathematics uses numbers instead of pictures.

What truly surprised him was that she'd talk to him at all. People rarely did and he'd liked it that way. He found people overwhelming—that's why he'd disappear into his art. It was his way to communicate with a world he couldn't completely understand and one that didn't understand him.

He'd found her to be an amusing nuisance. She'd peppered him with questions like a gnat, and showed him a childish drawing expecting him to praise it, which he had.

Then one day he realized she hadn't been trying to befriend him. She'd been mocking him.

The thought that he'd lowered his guard still irked him, but he wouldn't be fooled again. He knew what Bryant saw—a mildly interesting looking, brown skinned woman with shoulder length black hair she usually braided up into a bun, and passable attractive brown eyes—but he knew who she really was.

He'd let her try to have her way with his friend (and fail miserably because she really wasn't Bryant's type and he'd warned her) and then get things back to the way they were. The doctor said his wrist should recover well, he didn't want to think that he wouldn't be able to use his hand as before. What would he do if he couldn't create? Few things terrified him but the thought of the cast coming off and him not being as good as he'd once been haunted him.

"Why can't you do it?" Keeden asked just to needle his friend since he already knew the answer.

"Because I'm not that kind of artist."

"Neither is she."

"Which is exactly the kind of person we need. We don't need a professional. We need someone who won't go off and try to do their own vision, but will follow directions and mimic your style. She was trained in this particular craft. And it won't take long."

Keeden shook his head. "Your innate belief in people is nauseating."

Bryant smiled, this time for real. "It's the only way we've managed to stay friends this long."

"Friends?" Keeden scoffed. "I consider you more of a necessary evil."

Bryant laughed again, jumped up and kissed him on the cheek, which he knew—knew!—annoyed Keeden. "Which is why we're both rich and successful, I see opportunities you sometimes miss. Give her a chance. If it all goes pear-shaped I'll take responsibility."

Keeden wiped his cheek and shot his friend a measuring look. "And I'll take revenge."

12

―――――

"You're kidding, right?"

Maya continued to eat her stewed chicken and yellow rice as if no one had spoken. At least this time her sisters weren't laughing at her. Instead, they stared at her from across the dinner table as if she'd just levitated.

She'd pleased her parents by announcing she'd be leaving to start working at Keeden's place tomorrow. They'd left the table to go and make calls and assure the elders that everything was going as planned.

However, Ava and Cat had hardly touched their food. Or rather, Ava had hardly touched her food and Cat had hardly touched her second helping.

Cat had been the first to speak.

When Maya didn't reply, Ava leaned forward and gently said, "You two can't stand each other. Why would you agree to do this? You're going to hate every minute."

"No, I won't."

Cat narrowed her eyes. "What aren't you telling us?"

Ava turned to her. "What do you mean?"

Cat studied Maya. "She's hiding something."

Deceiving Cat had always been difficult. People underestimated her and she used it to her advantage. Maya knew better than to do that. "I have my own plan," she admitted.

"What is it?" Ava asked.

She couldn't stop a smile. "Bryant's going to be there."

Ava looked dismayed and Cat groaned.

"What?" Maya asked, surprised by their reactions. "I know it's a long shot, but I want to at least try."

They shared a look and Cat opened her mouth but Ava shook her head discouraging her.

"What?" Maya said annoyed by the silent conversation.

"Leave her alone, Cat. People can't help the way they feel."

"She should know who she's mooning over."

"I take offense to the word 'mooning,'" Maya said.

"Drooling then?"

"Withdraw the claws, Cat."

"I'm saying this because I love you."

"Go on," Maya said. "Tell me that he's too good for me. That I've made a fool of myself all these years that—"

"No, you're too good for him," Cat said in voice so fierce Maya blinked in surprise. "You're one of the few people who don't treat me like I'm invisible because I'm not beautiful like Gwen and Ava. You used to sketch me, remember? And you'd let me be your assistant when you went on trips to the museum or other art exhibitions. You stood up to Mom on our behalf. The moment you came to live with us was one of the happiest days of my life.

"You may be shorter than us but don't think we've ever stopped looking up to you. I don't want you to think you have to change for anyone. I don't think Bryant will ever be able to see how special you really are."

Maya sat back unable to know how to respond to such a

passionate speech. She'd never known her sisters thought of her like that. She blinked back tears.

"You don't see me as an unemployed failure?"

"No," Ava said. "You've lived life on your terms and we both admire you for that. We don't have the courage to."

Maya reached across the table and grabbed her sisters' hands. "My darling, darling girls," she said, using an affectionate term she'd used to call them anytime Gwen or their parents had said something to make them cry. For the first time she realized she truly had sisters she could depend on.

For a moment she wished she had the boldness to draw them as she truly saw them. Cat wasn't as plain and insignificant as others saw her and Ava wasn't the quiet, obedient woman everyone assumed her to be. But she also knew her sisters didn't see that about themselves yet and hoped one day they would. "Thank you for that. I needed it more than you know." She released their hands and sat back, sobering. "But I also know that...there are things about me that I have to work on." She needed to change, she wanted to change and this was her chance. "Ava's right, I can't help how I feel and I think Bryant's a wonderful man."

"But Bryant's not all that you think he is," Cat said.

"Does he have a secret family or something?"

"No," Cat said with a resigned sigh. "It's nothing like that."

Maya paused, a painful, worrying thought coming to her. "Do you...do you like him?"

For a moment Cat looked ill. "Not even close. I'm not warning you off because I'm jealous."

"Bryant is a good person," Ava said in a cautious tone. "We just don't want to see you get hurt."

"That's okay," Maya said relieved. "I'm used to getting hurt. That won't be anything new." She smiled at the worried looks on their faces. "But I love you two so much. I know that if it all ends in disaster I have two people I can depend on."

13

———

SOMEHOW MAYA never pictured a gorgeous stallion greeting her at the snake's den. She didn't know who she expected to open the ornate front door, a staff member perhaps, but she never imagined it to be Bryant. Her tongue felt heavy in her mouth. His smiled widened and the warmth in his gaze threatened to scorch her.

"I'm relieved," Bryant said, resting a hand on his broad chest with a sigh of relief. "I wasn't completely convinced you'd come."

For you I'd make my way through a snowstorm. Little did he know that she hadn't been able to come over fast enough. She'd over packed and had changed her hairstyle three times. Presently, she wore a headscarf because her last attempt, styling her braided hair into ringlets instead of letting them fall straight to her shoulders, had been a disaster.

She mutely smiled back.

"Of course she'd come," Keeden said in a deep mocking voice. "You're here after all."

Maya quickly fell from heaven into purgatory. She let her

gaze shift from Bryant's sweet, warm gaze to Keeden's cold, superior reptilian eyes and involuntarily shivered.

"Are you cold?" Bryant said.

"N-n-no," she said embarrassed he'd seen her reaction. "I...uh...I'm f-fine, thanks." She sent Keeden another glance, tamping down another visceral response of displeasure. He was dressed all in black—no surprise there—jeans and an overlong T-shirt. She still had a hard time believing he had a creative bone in his body. Perhaps his entire career was a sham. Perhaps he'd fooled the world and Bryant did all the work and Keeden got the credit. She could picture that. Bryant was the kind of man who didn't need the limelight. Keeden could easily manipulate others for his own benefit. But what she thought of him didn't matter.

She'd have to get used to being around him.

Three weeks.

She had three weeks to win over Bryant with this reptile's help and she wouldn't squander the opportunity.

"Can I take your bag?" Bryant said.

"N-no," Maya said quickly, gripping the strap tighter, not wanting him to realize that it would be bags, plural, and the carry-on she had over her shoulder, was just the beginning. "Please um...j-just show me the...uh...room."

"With pleasure," he said with a nod. His cell phone rang just as she closed the door. He checked the number and frowned. "Sorry, I have to take this." He looked at Keeden. "Fortunately, you're in good hands."

He left.

Maya felt as if she could breathe again. She sagged against the wall, but when she spotted Keeden's smug grin she straightened and said, "Just tell me where my room is and I'll find my way."

Keeden sighed. "I won't have you wandering around my house like a lost rat."

"Not a mouse?"

"Mice can be cute."

Which implied he didn't think she was. "True and snakes like to eat them."

He cast a look over her figure. "Only if they're small enough to swallow."

She rested a hand on her hip and cast a look over his body. "Only the weak ones would give up a tasty meal."

"And likely avoid indigestion." He sent a pointed look at her bag. "Do you have the entry fee?"

She made a face then unzipped her bag and pulled out the pastels. She held them out to him.

"Open it."

"You don't trust me?"

He blinked.

She swore and opened the container.

Keeden stepped forward and studied them, making her feel like a criminal doing a shady deal with a gangster. "They're all there," she said feeling both annoyed and anxious.

He trailed his hand along a row. "They're barely used."

Maya snapped the container closed, barely missing his fingers, and set it on the side table in the foyer. "Now we're even. Ready?"

He sent her an odd, considering look before he turned and headed up the stairs.

She reluctantly followed behind not wanting to be impressed but unable to help herself.

For a man who usually wore black she'd expected a cold, minimalist décor in grey and black.

Not a wooden staircase with sunflower yellow walls with red accents. She looked around, surprised by how nice and ordinary everything was. He was such an unpleasant person she'd expected his place to feel the same but it was strangely... comfortable. It must be the Bryant effect. He made everywhere he went seem ten times brighter and better.

The upper level split in two directions. They turned right and she noticed an L-shaped design with five doors bracketing a long hallway with glistening wood floors.

Keeden unceremoniously opened the first door. "Here. The bathroom's down the hall."

Maya stepped inside the room then stopped. She stared at the messy bed, the purple sweater carelessly tossed on a desk chair and male dress shoes near the closet. The place was clearly occupied. She turned to him in question.

Keeden grinned. "I thought you should get an idea of the layout of Bryant's bedroom in case you want to sneak in one night."

Maya raced out of the room and slammed the door shut. "What is wrong with you? Wait, no, don't answer that. I know what's wrong with you. You're an as—"

Keeden clicked his tongue. "No name calling. I was trying to be nice."

She marched ahead of him.

He grabbed her bag and pulled her back. "Your room isn't that way."

She gestured to the end of the hall. "That's yours, isn't it?"

He turned, pulling her with him. "Come on."

"I want to see your room first."

He pushed her ahead of him. "It's locked."

"No, it's not." She spun around him and raced to the door.

He raced after her and grabbed her arm just as she was reaching for the door handle. With his good hand he pulled her back with such force she stumbled into him and ended up elbowing him in the ribs. He grunted in pain and released her.

She turned and watched him stagger against the wall. He closed his eyes and rested his forehead against it clearly in agony.

"Why did you grab me?"

He didn't reply.

She softened her voice. "I'm sorry."

He kept his eyes closed. "Promise you won't go in my room."

"Like I said, I won't promise you anything, but I won't. You can relax." She hesitated. "Do you need to sit down? Do you need help? Do you want me to get Bryant?"

"I'm fine."

He didn't look fine. He looked as pale as he had been in the garden yesterday. "You shouldn't overexert yourself."

"I wasn't trying to."

She took a step towards him. "Do you need—?"

"I need you to stay away from me."

"I wish I could, but you're stuck with me for now." She took another step forward. "Anything you want me to do?"

"Stop breathing for starters."

She reached out and gently stroked his upper back, surprised that he let her and didn't pull away. He clearly was hurting more than he let on. Even his insult sounded more funny than biting. "You're sounding more like yourself already. Are you sure—?"

Keeden steadied himself against the wall then straightened. "I'm fine." He headed down the hall in the opposite direction of his bedroom. "Let me show you your room."

"It's on this floor?"

"Why wouldn't it be on this floor?"

"You didn't put me in the servants' quarters?"

He paused. "I had considered that as a second option."

She looked up at him curious. "What was your first?"

"The shed. Bryant talked me out of it."

She laughed.

"I'm serious."

"I know," Maya said amused. "That's why it's funny. You'd probably furnish it with a cot." When she saw a sly look cross his face, her brows shot up. "No, you'd think a cot was too good for me. You'd prefer me sleeping on the floor. A thin sleeping bag." She paused when he shook his head. "Not even a sleeping bag?"

"Two sheets."

She laughed again because it was exactly what she'd think of if she'd been in his position. "I'd at least offer you hay."

"Only because you think I lack the padding."

"That's true. A skinny thing like you might fall through one of the cracks."

He bit his lip. "Don't make me laugh."

He thought that was funny? Considering how much pain he'd been in only minutes ago, the fact oddly cheered her. "You're the one who started it."

He closed his eyes in regret. "I know."

She never thought he could have a sense of humor, especially when she teased him. He'd never found her funny before. He wasn't himself. He'd hit his head and was living on pain medicine that had briefly altered his personality. She'd enjoy it while it lasted. "Okay, show me to my broom cupboard."

"That was my third option."

She spun to him in surprise. "Seriously?"

"Yes."

"I bet the attic was the fourth option."

He shook his head. "I never considered the attic."

"Why not? Wait, I know. You'd never want me in a room above yours."

She laughed at the surprised look on his face. "You're so predictable."

"You'd think the same," he said.

"I'd stop at the broom cupboard, you'd easily fit in there."

"You can't fit me in a place you don't have."

Her good mood fell. Right, she didn't have a place of her own. Nice of him to remind her of their differences. He was rich and successful and she was...not.

Good, he just reminded her why she hated him, she'd briefly forgotten.

"...The space to fit me into. You'd have it too loaded with stuff."

She stared at him. He was right. If she did have a cupboard she would overstuff it. His pacing was off but he wasn't insulting her, he was...teasing her, but just a little delayed in responding, which surprised her that she'd noticed or cared. "Are you sure you're all right?"

Arctic eyes froze her in place. "I said I'm fine."

Yes, he was still as cuddly as a rattlesnake. He was okay.

14

———

THE HALLWAY FELT ENDLESS. Maya felt like they'd been walking for ages. She was certain they were miles away from his room. When would they reach hers? She stopped at a door and grabbed the handle. "Is this it?"

She began to open it but Keeden held it closed with the palm of his hand. "No." He gestured forward. "It's over there."

She nodded to the door he'd closed. "What's this?"

"Nothing." He shoved her forward.

"Can I at least see?"

"It's the linen closet." He opened the fourth door.

She looked at the bare bed with a stack of bed sheets in the middle. "Clearly do it yourself, huh?"

"I instructed the staff to treat you like a guest."

"Thank you."

"That I want to get rid of."

She started to laugh.

"You think that's funny?"

She set her bag on the bed and rubbed her hands together.

"Now I have an excuse to ask Bryant to my room. He can help me make my bed."

"I'd like to see you try."

"Making my own bed?"

"No, asking him to help you."

The jerk knew her mouth stopped working whenever Bryant was around. "Bastard."

"Coward."

He wasn't far from wrong. "Where's the studio?"

"You can see that later. Don't you want to get the rest of your things?"

"How do you know I have more bags?"

A quick grin came and went. "The look of panic on your face when Bryant offered to help you."

"I'll get them later."

Keeden leaned against the door. "Right. Under the cover of darkness so he can't see."

His accuracy was really starting to bug her. "Where is your studio?"

He frowned. "I said you'll see it later."

"I want to see it now."

"You should wait."

"I don't want to wait."

"Don't you want your beloved Bryant to show you? Isn't this the perfect chance to be alone with him?"

Of course she would prefer it but it made her more curious why Keeden hesitated to show her himself. "Why are you stalling?"

"I'm not stalling."

"Then let's go."

"This plan of yours won't work if you avoid him."

"I'm not avoiding anything, you are. Why don't you want to show me your studio?"

"I didn't say that."

"Then let's go."

He gazed out the window, absently rubbing his side.

"Are you hurting?"

He gritted his teeth. "Stop asking me that. I said I'm fine."

"Then prove it. Let's go."

He softly swore then left the room.

She followed him to the top of the stairs. He went down a few steps and she thought of the trick he'd played on her: Showing her Bryant's room first. Her mind remembering the sweater and shoes and the ruffled sheets that held his scent. Her cheeks still burned at the unintentionally intimate moment. How he delighted toying with her feelings. Stairs could be dangerous places.

Keeden suddenly paused and looked up at her. As if reading her mind, he suddenly said, "You first."

"Why?"

"I don't like the thought of you behind me."

"I wouldn't push you down the stairs."

"So you *were* thinking it."

Yes. "No."

"Yes, you were." Keeden motioned her forward. "Go ahead."

"How can I trust you won't push me?"

"Because I'm not violent."

"Neither am I."

He lifted up his cast. "I beg to differ."

"I didn't— Never mind. Okay, fine. If it makes you feel better." She brushed past him and briefly lost her footing. Her hand missed the railing and she would have tumbled down the stairs if Keeden hadn't grabbed her arm in a fierce grip that both shocked and steadied her.

She cleared her throat, her heart still pounding too fast. She noticed him unhook his other arm from the railing that had stopped them both from toppling down the stairs. He was stronger than he looked. "Thanks."

He abruptly released her and fire briefly melted his Arctic gaze. "You really are trying to kill me."

She noticed him gingerly touch his side. "Did I hurt you?"

His eyes flashed. "I changed my mind," he said, moving past her. "You're too clumsy to push anything down the stairs."

She glared at the back of his head. Just when she thought he was partially human he reminded her he was a prick.

When they reached the main floor, Keeden turned to her with an expression of a man facing torture by a thousand beestings. "I think you should wait for Bryant—"

Maya opened her mouth to agree with him when Bryant appeared in the hallway coming from the living room and said, "Are we all set?"

"Yes," Keeden said. "You can show her the studio. She's eager to see it." He turned and left.

Maya watched him go, suspicious. Only seconds before he'd seemed tolerable and then he turned cold. Why didn't he want to show her the studio? "What was that?"

"He's shy."

Maya turned back to Bryant certain he was joking. Keeden? Shy? She couldn't imagine it. "He just got tired of my company."

"No, that's not it."

She wouldn't argue. She'd never managed to argue with Bryant. If he wanted to protect his friend she'd let him. She'd be careful not to criticize Keeden in Bryant's presence. "Y-you're probably right. He...uh...he's probably hurting." She briefly considered telling him how she'd accidentally elbowed Keeden and then how he'd had to save her from falling down the stairs then thought better of it. It didn't put her in a good light. "You'd better check on him later."

He nodded. "I will."

He studied her and her hand went to her headscarf wondering if it was crooked or messy or...

"I really appreciate you doing this," he said.

Oh God, he was close and smiling at her and her mouth wouldn't move. All she could manage was a strangled giggle. To her relief he turned and she followed behind him, silently berating herself for her silly behavior. She had to get a grip. She didn't want to continue to be the coward Keeden thought she was.

"I-I'm ready to...uh...tackle whatever you give me."

"That's the spirit. We both know Keeden can be grumpy, so I'm glad you're overlooking it. You're really helping us out of a bind. He wouldn't want me to tell you this but this project has been a struggle for him. So if you have any suggestions feel free to share."

No way. Keeden would never want to hear what she'd have to say and she doubted she'd have anything to offer him. But Bryant appeared to be serious and seemed to be waiting for a response from her so she plastered on a smile and said, "Um...r-right. Sure."

"I mean it. He needs this to work. He's been in a bit of a slump."

Maya felt like covering her ears. This was too much information. Didn't Bryant realize how much she and Keeden couldn't stand each other? Was it really fair to Keeden for Bryant to share his weakness like this? This was a man whose work was in galleries across the globe. He was supposed to be impenetrable.

She didn't like the man, but learning this information about him, instead of making her feel smug, embarrassed her. It made him sound a little too human for her liking. But Bryant was too sweet and naïve to understand how dark her thoughts could be against his best friend. He was completely unaware of the ammunition he was giving her.

"See, after his mother died—"

No, no, no. She definitely didn't want to know this. "Well, I'll do my best to help," Maya interrupted, surprised she'd managed to do so without stumbling over her words. "And the s-sooner I get started the s-sooner we...uh...can finish."

He nodded and headed towards the east wing of the grand house, telling her about Keeden and how hard he'd worked to achieve his success that others only deemed as luck. Maya pretended to listen (she didn't really care that at the beginning of his career Keeden had travel to whatever small gallery would show his work and paid his own way before his work gained notice) as she followed Bryant through a series of rooms and a long winding path before they made it to the back of the house, crossed a short window bracketed hallway and stopped in front of the studio door.

She felt as if Bryant had taken a longer way round but quickly brushed the thought aside, finding no reason why he would have done so.

He opened the door and motioned her inside.

The house had been surprising but this room. This room was astounding. Bright, beautiful. For such a dark figure, it was like discovering a vampire had a soft spot for kittens.

15

———

It felt like hours before he heard footsteps.

"You can stop hiding," Bryant said.

Keeden sighed. "I wasn't hiding."

Bryant looked around the walk-in closet where he'd found his friend sitting on a stool staring at a row of shoes. "You're literally in the farthest corner of your closet."

"It's a walk-in."

"It's still a closet."

He noticed Keeden tucking his cell phone away and folded his arms. "Have you been texting Amata behind my back?"

Bryant enjoyed pretending to be jealous of Keeden's friendship with Amata Diaz, a modern dance teacher in her fifties. A car accident in her thirties that had left her paralyzed from the waist down could have derailed her career. Instead, with the support of her husband and family she opened a studio and still choreographed dances and taught.

She had helped him get over his grief when he'd stumbled into her studio at fifteen years old after missing the afterschool bus. He'd walked a couple of block heading for a convenience store before he rushed into the studio to avoid getting soaked in the unexpected downpour.

The sound of the lyrical jazz music hit him first before he noticed the woman in the wheelchair moving her arms high with power and command.

He'd watched her transfixed, his artistic eye seeing colors as well as movement as she filled the space, and stirred a longing within him, a longing to connect to something beautiful instead of the anger and sadness that continued to grip him.

He kept coming back and, to her credit, she didn't tell him to leave. Weeks later he gained the boldness to ask for lessons in exchange for cleaning up the studio, knowing his father wouldn't pay for them.

She agreed and helped him develop core strength, stamina, power of movement—which later came in handy—and healthy ways to deal with his feelings. She'd helped him get out of his head.

Even more important she'd taught him how to fall. It was due to her constant training, and his years of staying fit, that he'd automatically let his body respond in the way it needed to and not stiffen and resist when the car hit him, otherwise he might have been more injured. He'd teased her that she'd saved his life.

"It's no secret I love her more than you."

Bryant looked briefly pained but the expression quickly passed. "So why are you hiding?"

"I'm not hiding. I'm...getting space. Did that idiot tell you she—"

"She what?" Bryant urged when Keeden abruptly stopped talking.

"Nothing." He'd keep her nearly falling down the stairs a secret, although he was certain she'd shaved off another year off of his life. He also wouldn't tell his friend he'd needed to get as far away from her as he could.

Just for a few minutes to recover from the fact that she'd nearly made him laugh. That being in her company hadn't been as horrendous as he'd pictured it. She'd laughed more than he'd thought she would and he liked the sound. But Bryant didn't need to know any of that. If he wanted to get Maya out of his house, he had to help her get Bryant to see her in another light. Of course he'd have to work on not calling her an idiot.

"Come downstairs."

He didn't move. He was afraid to. Ashamed by how his heart raced at the question bubbling up his throat. He didn't want to ask it. It made him sound pathetic but he had to know. He trailed the length of his cast with his forefinger. "Did you show her the studio?"

"Yeah."

He swallowed. "Did she laugh?"

"No."

He let his hand fall and looked up at his friend surprised. "Really?"

Bryant nodded. "Really."

Keeden studied his face sure he was keeping something back. "But she made a snarky comment, right?"

"No."

Keeden felt his heart lift then slowly sink. He rolled his eyes. What was he getting happy about? Of course she wouldn't. Maya could barely form words around Bryant. She probably just smiled like an idiot—he'd really have to work on not calling her that—and would save her caustic comments for him.

And he didn't want to hear them. Which is why he was in his closet staring at his shoes because he was too sensitive. He cared too much. He didn't want to care, he didn't want her opinion (or anyone's opinion) to matter to him, but no matter what armor he built around himself he had soft spots.

Spots she could cause to bleed and he wasn't in the mood to fight.

His studio was important to him and to have that woman in it...

He knew that soon he'd have to face the torment of hearing her judgment, he'd come up with a ready reply, he'd gotten good at it, but battle with her still left him wounded. She knew how to get to his core.

He hated that.

Growing up he'd endured bullying (busted lips and black eyes before he learned to fight back) and his father's disdain but Maya got to him like no one else could.

He'd do his best to make sure their schedules didn't cross. How, he wasn't sure yet, but he'd figure out something. He didn't want to be in there alone with her. He'd give her the assignment then stay away until she was done. He'd come up with certain hours so they'd barely need to see each other. He'd—

"She said it was amazing."

"Who?" Keeden said, slowly coming out of his thoughts. He kept his voice and gaze lowered.

"Maya. She said the studio was amazing."

His head snapped up. "No, she didn't."

"Yes, she did."

"You're lying."

"You're right."

"I knew it. What did she really say?" He steeled himself.

"She said it was spectacular, amazing, beautiful, one of the most awe-inspiring studio she'd ever seen."

"Now you're exaggerating."

"I'm not."

Then she was lying of course. Lying to impress Bryant. But damn why did her words make him happy? He wished he hadn't for a second felt...damn, he didn't want to feel anything with regard to her, let alone a feeling of pride. The problem was she pushed all the wrong buttons with him. Usually people didn't get to him. He'd had to develop the hide of a rhino to make it as an artist and yet this art professor knew how to make him feel small.

That silly string bean? Isn't he funny? That's what he'd overheard her calling him at one party. He'd trusted her and she'd been laughing and mocking him behind his back the entire time. *Silly string bean.* The memory still burned. He'd been especially sensitive about his looks back then and had been fair game for lots of teasing (once getting strung up by his underwear on a hook in the boy's locker room) because of how small and skinny he was. But he'd thought she was different. She would not make a fool of him again.

Her opinion must not matter whether it was a lie or truth.

"Where is she now?" he asked.

"She's still there."

Keeden shot to his feet in alarm. "What?"

"She's still there," Bryant calmly repeated.

"You left her alone in the studio?"

"Yes, she wanted to look around."

"I never leave anyone alone in there."

"You never *let* anyone in there."

"Exactly and I have my reasons. People like to touch things, shift this, peek, sneak. She could be taking pictures and posting them online or something."

"I told her not to do that."

"Really?"

Bryant laughed. "No."

"It's not funny."

"Why would she do that?"

"Because she hates me." Keeden dashed out of the room and down the stairs, ignoring the pain he felt doing so, and ignoring Bryant calling after him to be careful.

This was probably his fault. He should have showed her the studio when she'd first asked him then he could have hustled her through, showed her the basics and controlled what she saw. He certainly wouldn't have left her there alone.

This arrangement was already proving to be a disaster. He knew this wouldn't work. She was already a nuisance. She'd probably already tidied up what she'd see as a mess and what he saw as freedom. She'd likely have lots of corrections to make. Unnecessary opinions that he'd have to pretend didn't bother him.

Keeden ran through the open door—Bryant had left it open?—and found Maya sitting at one of the workstations. He had three of them: One where he did his sketches, carvings and paintings, another for digital work and the last was in the far corner of the large space for non-commissioned projects.

Of course she was sitting at that one, giving her a chance to pry into one of his most sacred works.

16

Maya sat on one of the stools with one hand cupping her chin, looking as bored as a teenager being lectured about the 'facts of life' as she stared at the project that Keeden hadn't told anyone about. It was too late to stop her from unseeing it.

He briefly rested against the doorframe letting his body recover from his crazy, mad run. But adrenalin seemed to keep any pain signals at bay because all he felt was anger. It coursed through his veins.

When he felt steady enough, he took a step forward trying to think of the best way to stop her from looking at his special project anymore, but then got distracted by a rainbow of color bouncing off the walls. He looked up and saw the hanging crystal and glass sculpture he had hung in the center of the room. It had four more spherical crystals that hadn't been there before. They'd fallen after a storm and he hadn't had a chance to replace them. But she had?

No, that had to have been Bryant. As short as Maya was she'd have had to get on a ladder and then use metal pliers to fashion the crystals back in place. She'd probably found the sculpture ridiculous and gaudy as well as the rest of his studio that his father, a prominent ophthalmologist, had once described as "childish." He had urged Keeden to make it look more professional to resemble the other studios he'd seen in magazines: Ones with complementary colors and not a big yellow starburst on the ground and an assortment of African masks lining the walls. But Keeden had designed the studio to suit his tastes, as eccentric as they may be.

Keeden shifted his gaze from the sculpture and suddenly noticed two things: One, nothing had been touched. That was a relief. Everything was in its rightful, juxtaposed place. Two, the place felt oddly calm. Usually when anyone was exposed to his work he felt a sense of anxious, shimmering chaos, but he didn't sense that with her there (and he should since she was chaos personified).

He gripped his hand into a fist. None of that mattered.

He had to get her away from that table.

He took a step forward.

She looks interested.

It was a wayward thought he quickly pressed down. True, he didn't see a critical smirk of judgment on her face but that didn't mean anything. He couldn't let it mean anything.

You know you're curious about what she thinks.

No, no, no. No, he wouldn't ask what she thought of the story he'd been working on. He'd had more than enough of her today. He still had to get over her lying about how much she liked his studio in order to impress Bryant. Knowing her, stringing that many words together must have been a task.

But that didn't matter now. The project she continued to study, like a professor ready to offer a critique, was unfinished and he'd likely never show it to anyone anyway. He wasn't known for illustrated stories (Bryant was the writer) and didn't feel he was very good at them. He'd done it as a lark to try something new. Recently, he felt his work had a dangerous sameness and he was becoming restless and bored with his success. He was known for abstract works, some surrealism, mixed media projects, glass works, woodblocks, and patterns some of which he licensed to different manufacturers of fabrics and furniture.

People kept wanting the same thing from him. He was starting to feel more like a manager in a factory than an artist. The joy he'd once had wasn't there. He didn't feel like himself anymore, but an empty replica that the world applauded but he secretly abhorred.

He'd struggled for years to become a known gallery artist then achieved that dream and taken on commissioned work. After achieving that goal, he'd started the business with Bryant and made money off of products he'd developed or licensed and still took on other projects, but now felt listless. He didn't know what to do with himself.

Until this story had gripped him.

It had pulled him out of his sleep one night and he'd rushed to his studio and drafted the main images and ideas that filled his mind then feverishly worked on it for days.

And then...

And then hit a wall. He didn't know how to fix it. He knew he wasn't good with words like Bryant but he'd still wanted to make the effort even if it was a complete failure.

He just didn't enjoy his enemy sitting at the table to witness it.

"So how does it end?"

Maya hadn't lifted her head and her words sounded so normal that Keeden wasn't sure she'd actually spoken to him.

Whenever she did there was always a cutting, biting quality. But it was as if curiosity had softened her tone.

He felt bare, exposed, for a wild instant he wanted to run forward and jump on the table and cover his work with his body. But it was too late. She'd seen everything already. "I don't know yet."

She nodded before she finally looked up at him. "Well, it has to be happy."

He frowned. "No it doesn't."

"Yes it does."

He scratched his cheek. "Just because there are pictures doesn't mean it's a kid's book. It's—" He stopped when she stuck her tongue out at him. Keeden was so stunned by the juvenile display that he stood with his mouth open.

Maya returned her gaze to the pictures.

"Did you just stick your tongue out at me?"

She slowly turned to him and did it again.

He pointed at her. "Stop that."

"Then stop being a dummy."

"A dummy?"

"Of course I know this book isn't for children," she said. "I took a course on comic and graphic novel design."

In spite of himself he took an eager step forward. "You did?"

"Yes, I learned the power of metaphor, composition, marrying text with imagery. So many wonderful things." She wagged her finger at him. "And I'm not going to tell you a single thing I learned."

Damn, he deserved that. Didn't matter, he didn't need her help anyway. He'd find his way on his own.

"It doesn't have to be a happy ending," he said.

"But the way you've structured it, it isn't tragic enough.

You'll disappoint the reader. It's a story composed of symbols. The poor dog locked out in the rain and his valiant..."

"Valiant?"

"...struggles to reunite with his family. I don't know how you'll do it but he must succeed."

"Why?"

"Because that's where he belongs."

"Maybe he doesn't. Maybe he needs to find somewhere else to be. Another family."

Maya shook her head. "No, like I said, it's not that kind of story. It doesn't end in death and he doesn't end up alone."

He had considered those two options. He felt it would give the story depth, but he wondered if that was also why he'd been struggling with it. However, a happy ending felt too pat too predictable and not like him.

"How would you end it?"

"I told you. Happy."

Unfortunately, that didn't mean anything to him. "Happy how?"

"It doesn't matter. It's your story not mine. Just make sure it's happy. Whatever happiness looks like to you, that'll be the ending it needs."

She slid off the stool. "So what do you need me to do?"

She'd ended the discussion and he was glad. Sort of. Part of him liked debating with her. Strangely, she'd seen something he hadn't. The story as a metaphor and she hadn't laughed. He cautiously stepped farther into the room. The room was big but not big enough to make him feel comfortable with her in it.

"I've got a woodblock print project I've been working on. I need these carved." He gestured to the wood pieces lined on a long counter against the wall. "And if you say a computer can simulate this effect I will banish you from here."

"What's the point of stating the obvious?"

"Go on and say it."

"What?"

He gestured to the room. "Bryant isn't here so you don't have to pretend anymore. You think I'm ridiculous."

She sent him a curious look. "Yes. Again, why state the obvious?"

Now they were getting somewhere. Here would come the insults. "And you think this room is childish, banal, overwrought rubbish."

Keeden steeled himself for a raised chin, a glint in her eyes before her acid tongue shot its poison.

Instead Maya looked hurt. "Why would I think that? Oh, is it because you think I'm too stupid to see the atmospheric design you were going for?"

His heart constricted at the expression. He hadn't expected to hurt her. "No."

"I'm just a dumb teacher so of course I don't have the superior artistic eye to see anything worthy of notice. Why would a plebian like me see anything, right?"

Keeden stared at her stunned. No, wait. This wasn't how they played this game.

"Even when I'm trying to be nice you can't miss an opportunity to put me down," Maya said with a reluctant sigh. "To put me in my place." She softly swore before she mumbled, "I shouldn't have let Bryant get to me. I shouldn't have listened to him. I know what you're really like." She raised her voice and looked at him. "I'll always be an easy target for you."

For a moment Keeden felt ill. She was supposed to look angry, irritated not hurt. She knew the rules. He threw a verbal punch and she punched back or vice versa. He'd never wounded her before. The thought unnerved him. "So you really like it?"

He hated how vulnerable he sounded, but he had to know.

"Yes," she said acid back in her tone.

"Maya, I—"

"And I'm so disappointed that this amazing studio belongs to a jerk like you that I might actually cry. I can't be in here anymore. I'll start working tomorrow." She ran out of the room but not before he caught the sight of her tears.

17

———

KEEDEN COLLAPSED onto the stool Maya had abandoned, feeling as if he'd been hit by an avalanche.

Something had just happened and he didn't know what. He couldn't interpret it. The Maya who had just raced out of his studio was not the Maya he knew. That Maya was a stranger, as was the one who'd also made him laugh, the one who'd assessed his unfinished story and debated him, challenged him. Did she want to impress Bryant so much that she'd changed her personality? Or did she want to butter Keeden up so that he'd hold up his end of the bargain? Didn't she know that he'd help her anyway? The sooner she was gone the better. She didn't have to pretend to be nice to him.

But what truly disturbed him was that she didn't seem to be pretending. Her words and actions seemed genuine. Even the interested look in her eyes. He'd wanted to talk to her more.

That had never happened before.

Well, it had happened years ago before he discovered the truth about how she felt about him. But not since then.

What the hell was going on?

Keeden jumped when he heard the door slam. He looked up and saw Bryant. And from the look on his friend's face he'd royally messed up.

Bryant wasn't smiling.

When Bryant didn't smile that meant trouble. Bryant usually had a welcoming grin, a devious smirk, a broad smile or a sly quirk. It was his trademark.

But at that moment there was no trace of it.

He looked furious. That was the look Keeden had expected from Maya, not his friend. This was proof his world had been flipped upside down.

Bryant march over to him and did one of the few things Keeden detested. He folded his arms and stared him down.

They used to do it in college. Keeden usually won, he could outstare anyone, but this time there was something so dark in his friend's gaze and Keeden felt shaken from Maya's uncharacteristic behavior that after a few seconds he had to look away.

He swore and sat back down. "Just say it."

His friend remained silent.

He shot him a look. "I mean it."

"I'm trying to figure out..."

Keeden stood. "Figure it out on your own time."

Bryant pushed him back down. "Don't make me regret knowing you." His arms fell to his sides. "I spent nearly ten mintues singing your praises. Buttering her up so she'd see you in a different light and you destroy it in two seconds." He threw his arms out to the side. "It's just a bloody room."

Keeden blinked. That was not what he'd expected him to say. "What?"

"If you want to get angry at someone take it out on me not her."

Keeden opened his mouth then closed it not knowing what

to say. His mind racing. Everything felt topsy-turvy. Chaos. The woman was chaos.

Bryant rested his hands on his hips. "What the hell did you say to her?"

"I don't know."

"Don't give me that. You don't hurt someone like that and not know what you did."

"I didn't mean to hurt her. I thought when you told me what she said about the studio that she was lying."

"Why would she lie?"

Because she likes you and hates me that's why! That was the natural order of things.

Keeden briefly closed his eyes, feeling the world spinning. This was too much stimulation. He felt emotionally worn. "I don't know," he said in a quiet voice. "I honestly don't know."

"Do you think she'd have fixed your sculpture if she was lying?"

So she had been the one to repair the damage and Bryant had helped her.

She'd probably done it to impress Bryant, but now Keeden wasn't so sure. His mouth suddenly felt dry. "I didn't mean to hurt her." It was the truth even though he knew neither would believe him.

"If you want this to work, you'd better apologize."

No, he didn't want to face her right now. He shifted in his seat, traced an image with his finger. "I think it'd be better if you do it. You're always my good manners."

"No."

He traced another image. He knew how to get to Bryant. His friend had a soft heart and if he kept his tone quiet and humble enough his friend would cave. "I really messed up. We both know it'd sound more sincere coming from you. Flash one of your smiles and she'll be putty in your hands."

Bryant continued to stare at him unmoved.

"I mean it. You should check on her. See if she's okay." She'd love that: Bryant going to her in a moment of need, caring about her. This would be a perfect way to make it up to her. "Please. I know I'm the last person she wants to see right now and...and I might say something and make it worse."

Bryant hesitated.

Keeden bit his lip. His friend was wavering. With one nudge he'd fall. "I'm begging you."

Bryant relented and nodded. "Fine."

Keeden inwardly cheered his success.

"But only this once," he called over his shoulder as he walked to the door.

"While you're at it, thank her for fixing the sculpture too."

Bryant stopped in the doorway and turned to him. He didn't smile, which meant Keeden would have to find a way to make it up to his friend too, but he didn't look as furious as before. "I'll apologize for you," he said, "but you'll have to thank her yourself."

18

———

"*That dress looks so good on you.*"

Maya listened to the soft sound as the ASMR artist stroked her hand over the velvet material. It was the second video she'd watched. She didn't usually get her fix in the daytime, preferring it as a nighttime meditation but Keeden had so infuriated her she'd been forced to break her routine.

After dealing with his insults Maya had run into her room and locked the door, ashamed the threat of tears had been real. She'd barely left the studio before they began flowing like a waterfall down her cheeks. She'd bumped into Bryant in the hall before she reached the stairs and he'd called out her name, but she'd raced passed him. It was doubly humiliating to let him see her like that, but at least the jerk hadn't. She hadn't given him that satisfaction.

The sobs hit the moment she closed the door.

Everything that had happened was too reminiscent of that day. That horrible day and his cold words.

Words she'd feared were true.

Those who can, do. Those who can't, teach.

Keeden had sliced her in two with everyone—her parents, her half-sisters, the elders—watching, and left her a laughing-stock. She wanted to block out the still hauntingly painful memory so she'd grabbed her cell phone. She would have buried herself under the sheets, but, of course, the bed was unmade. So she'd had to grab a sheet and wrap it around herself, briefly annoyed by how soft the fabric was when it brushed against her cheek(the bastard had good taste), and jumped on the bed and started watching videos.

Sounds of comfort. A way to escape. In this other place she belonged. She could pretend someone was happy to see her, that they truly cared.

"How about a scarf?" the ASMR artist continued.

That jerk. She knew she shouldn't have let her guard down. Why had she listened to Bryant telling her about how much Mr. Adesina hadn't supported his son's dream?

Why had she thought the man who'd created such a creative, touching yet simple tale could be kind? There were plenty of artists who created brilliant works who were tyrants underneath.

"Maya?"

She froze. Bryant. He was knocking on her door. He was calling her name. For years this had been a dream of hers.

Why did it suddenly feel like a nightmare? She sniffed and touched her tear stained cheeks. This was not how she'd pictured it. Her heart began to pound. If she stayed really still perhaps he'd go away...

"Maya, I know you're in there. I can hear you listening to something."

She swore. She'd kept the volume on her cell phone too high. She hadn't been thinking.

She couldn't tell him to go away. She could never do that.

"I really want to talk to you," he said. "I won't take long, but it's important that I do and not through the door like this."

Damn.

He wasn't going to leave. "Uh...give m-me a...uh...minute." She jumped up and stared at herself in the vanity mirror.

She suppressed a scream at the sight of her red, puffy eyes. Her hand flew to her head. And when did she lose her headscarf? Her wayward hair sprung up all over her head like vines. She could not let him see her like that. "Um...my room is a...um...mess could we uh talk s-somewhere else?"

"The garden—"

"Not the garden." She squeezed her eyes shut, wishing she hadn't sounded so sharp. "I-I mean...if y-you don't mind."

"I don't. I'll just meet you on the patio when you're ready. Five minutes enough?"

No. "Okay." She heard his footsteps fade away.

She opened her bag glad she'd grabbed the one with a pair of sunglasses. That would hide her eyes, now she had to do something about her hair, but she didn't have time.

Maya crept to the door and slowly opened it. The hallway was empty.

Good.

She tiptoed out of her room and went to the foot of the stairs. That's when she saw her lost headscarf, on the ground, hanging off one of the railing balusters. She hurried down the stairs and grabbed it. Victory.

Now all she had to do was rewrap her hair, perhaps put some lipstick on and then she'd be ready for Bryant.

She hurried up the stairs then stopped when a figure appeared at the top: Keeden.

She stared up at him.

He stared down at her.

She gripped the railing.

He held out his good hand.

"I'm not going to fall," she said, surprised she could manage words.

"I know that. Give me the scarf."

She held it protectively close. "I need it."

"I know," he said impatiently. "He won't wait forever. You need to do something with your hair, unless you want to turn him into stone."

Medusa. He was comparing her to a monster with snakes on her head.

He took her moment of outrage to grab the scarf, spin her around and quickly wrap her hair. "You look good, now wait a minute."

She turned to say something to him, meet his eyes, but his gaze was fixated on the ground as he rummaged in his jeans pocket. He pulled out a bracelet and pair of hanging earrings. "Here." When she stared at the objects, he impatiently said, "Bryant likes gold."

She slid on the bracelet then took the earrings. "Did you design these?"

"My sister left them on her last visit," Keeden said, which didn't answer her question and she had a sneaking suspicion he didn't plan to.

He unceremoniously turned and walked away. She put on the earrings then marched down the stairs, the farther away she was from him the better.

BRYANT STOOD up when he saw her. He smiled. His beauty competing with the brightness of the sun.

"You really had me worried but then you waltz out here looking like a movie star." He pulled out one of the seven tan colored chairs surrounding the long rectangular table.

"A movie star?"

"With the sunglasses and how you styled your hair. I'm glad Keeden didn't rattle you too much."

Maya tried to see her reflection in the window but only saw a blurred image. But as long as Bryant was impressed it didn't matter who had done her hair.

Bryant poured her some raspberry lemonade. "He's the reason I wanted to talk to you." He sighed. "He's not the easiest man to get along with but he does need your help."

"I uh won't quit if t-that's um uh what you're worried about."

"I am, but also...he didn't mean to hurt you. Whatever he said he's sorry. He took the coward's way out and wanted me to tell you. He was insistent saying you'd take it better from me than him."

He was right. Sort of. In the past she would have cherished this moment. She was alone with Bryant, and he was smiling at her and looking sincere and concerned on her behalf and yet...

And yet she felt a sense of disappointment that Keeden hadn't apologized himself.

She thought about their encounter on the stairs. His eyes had been guarded rather than cold and comparing her to Medusa had more of a teasing tone than a brutal criticism. He'd actually helped her.

No one had helped her like that before. Her mother deemed her useless and Ava and Cat, at first, were too young (being seven and eight years her junior) and then she left home at nineteen and was too focused on her studies and being a broke student to focus on her looks. In later years, if her sisters offered to help her, she never gave them the chance. It felt too embarrassing. They didn't struggle with styling the way she did.

But quickly and efficiently Keeden had styled her hair and made her look good for Bryant. So good that Bryant had actually complimented her. And the feeling felt so strange, surreal, but instead of basking in it she wanted to get a mirror and see what Keeden had done.

"...if you want—"

"Will you excuse me for a minute?" Maya interrupted, feeling ashamed that she hadn't been listening to him but knowing that her curiosity was only growing. "I'll be right back."

She raced into the powder room, took off her sunglasses and stared at her reflection in the mirror.

She gasped.

This time she didn't look like a nightmare.

This time she looked like a stylish figure. How had Keeden managed to get that effect with a headscarf and only the use of one hand? The way he twisted the fabric allowed the pattern of the cloth to both sculpt her head and give her height. And the earrings and bracelet, instead of overwhelming her short neck, chubby wrist and round face, complimented them.

He was too much of a coward to apologize himself.

She knew this act had been his apology and in an instant she was able to forgive him. *Dumb jerk,* she muttered feeling better.

"Are you okay?" Bryant asked when Maya returned to the table.

"Yes, I'm fine and it's okay. You don't need to be Keeden's good manners. I'll know how to handle him from now on."

Bryant looked relieved. "I'm glad to hear that."

Maya lifted her glass and took a sip before she smiled. "Me too."

19

UNDER THE COVER OF DARKNESS.

Maya thought of Keeden's words as she carried her last bag to her bedroom undetected by Bryant or any household staff.

The house remained quiet and still as evening settled, cocooning the house in a soft pink and purple haze.

After enjoying a delicious chef-prepared dinner of spicy fish and brown rice while Bryant made her laugh—and Maya still not able to form coherent sentences (she really had to work on that)—she'd disappeared into her room and taken the opportunity to get the rest of her things.

She hadn't seen Keeden for hours.

"He likes to keep odd hours," Bryant had told her at dinner, which they ate on the patio, a soft breeze carrying the scent of the lime accent in the meal. She'd asked (only out of politeness) if Keeden was going to join them. "Don't worry," Bryant assured her. "You probably won't see him the rest of the day. You're safe until tomorrow."

She thanked him, still struggling to remember how to talk and swallow, but also feeling a little guilty. It wasn't that she was trying to find out Keeden's schedule in order to avoid him. She was truly curious.

Which made no sense at all.

Maya set the last bag on the bed and sighed. Instead of asking Bryant to help her (as Keeden had rightly guessed she wouldn't) she'd made her own bed.

At least she'd begun to until she'd gotten distracted by the luxurious feel of the plum purple sheets as she stretched them over the queen sized mattress. She didn't know linens could feel so soft, then she touched the towels and felt certain Keeden'd had someone pluck them from the softest cloud in the sky. Her bare feet nestled into the soft cushioned light purple rug, stretching out from under the bed. It was layered on top of the grey carpet, cleverly drawing one's gaze to the focal point in the eggshell grey room.

Keeden might have wanted to inconvenience her but giving her sheets, towels and carpeting infused with elegance and designed for pleasure was a temptation instead of a deterrent. She'd tease him about them later.

After she finally managed to finish making the bed and putting some of her things away, she decided to head to the kitchen for a snack.

She saw a splash of light seeping from the living room and peeked her head inside.

She saw Keeden sitting on the dark grey couch under one lit lamplight. Four large windows with their long maroon colored drapes still open, stared back at her like two pairs of dark eyes.

He wasn't doing anything—not watching something on his cell phone or the flat screen TV or reading. He just sat staring ahead. Perhaps he was meditating?

"What do you want?" he said.

Her initial instinct was to step back and pretend she hadn't seen him. That she hadn't been spying on him like some kid waiting up to see if Santa Claus was real. She didn't know why she hadn't gone straight to the kitchen as she'd planned to. But she couldn't tell him that. She had to come up with a reason she'd been staring.

Maya looked down at the bracelet he'd given her. She quickly took it off and the earrings too. She walked into the room and held them out to him. "Here."

He didn't look at her. "Keep them."

"I thought you said they belonged to your sister."

"Not anymore. Now they're yours."

"But you said she left them behind."

Keeden released a tired sigh. "Do you like them or not?"

"I do."

"Then they're yours."

"Are you sure she won't mind?"

He finally looked at her. "Does that really bother you?"

"Of course. I can just picture being summoned to another meeting." She mimicked Papa So and So's deep baritone. "The Kayodes and Adesinas have known each other for centuries. Thievery has never marred our name." She changed her tone. "And I'd say, 'But Keeden said I could have them' and then Aunty Such and Such would say 'Melody Adesina is in tears accusing you of taking what belonged to her' and I'd say 'He said she wouldn't mind' and your sister would deny it and then —" Maya stopped when she noticed him staring at her amused. "I'm making too big a deal of this, aren't I?"

"As always."

"Easy for you to be so nonchalant about it. You don't know what it's like not to be given the benefit of the doubt. People tend to think the worst of me, present company included."

Keeden nodded before he said, "If there's any trouble with the jewelry come to me."

That made her feel better. People tended to doubt her word but not his. "Thanks."

"Thank you."

"For what?"

He cleared his throat. Scratched his chin. Cleared his throat again. "The uh...sculpture."

"Oh, you're welcome."

"But be careful next time. It's really high up."

She sniffed. "Then you should be encouraging me."

"Why would I do that?"

"I could lose my balance and fall and break a leg then you'd be rid of me."

"That wouldn't happen."

"Why not?"

"Because Bryant would be there to catch you."

She felt her cheeks heat. Instead of being cheered by the scenario it embarrassed her. "I wouldn't want that."

"Why not?"

She wasn't going to tell him that she didn't want Bryant to see her as a klutz. It was bad enough having Keeden see her that way. "Just because. Anyway, you don't need to worry about me. Bryant was holding the ladder. I felt fine. And even though you've probably heard it hundreds of times and my lowly opinion means nothing to you, I think that sculpture is extraordinary."

"Hmmm."

She pointed to the windows. "Do you want me to close the drapes?"

"No."

She should leave. She knew she should leave but she didn't feel like it yet. She wondered where he'd disappeared to for the rest of the day, but she wouldn't ask that. Instead she stalled by putting on the bracelet and earrings. "So what are you doing here?"

"Nothing."

"You're doing nothing?"

He nodded.

"How can you do that?"

Keeden sent her a long look. "It's really simple," he said slowly. "You sit down and do nothing."

"I don't think I could manage that."

"No, you couldn't."

"Is that a challenge?"

"That's a statement of fact."

Maya sat down on the other end of the couch. She didn't want to face him, she'd find that too distracting and intimidating, especially when trying something she'd never done before. "I can try." She clasped her hands together. "So what's the first step?"

"You just did it."

"I did? Oh, right. Sitting down. And then what?"

"Nothing."

"I just sit here?"

He nodded.

"And do nothing?"

He pinched the bridge of his nose.

Maya read the pained expression. "And that includes no talking, right?"

"Maya," Keeden said with thinning patience, "don't torture yourself."

"No," she said as she settled back into her seat. "I want to try."

She lasted twenty seconds before she started fidgeting, a minute before she began to swing her foot then another thirty seconds before she said, "Are you sure you're not meditating?"

"I'm not meditating."

"You're not visualizing or repeating a mantra in your mind?"

"I'm not doing anything."

"You're just sitting there."

"Yes."

"Why?"

"Because it calms me." He turned fully to her. "At least it used to."

She held up her hands. "Okay, I won't bother you. I'll get this right. I'll be calm. Perfectly calm. And I'll—"

"*Nothing* includes no talking."

"Right." Maya took a deep breath. Keeden made it look so easy. She could do this. She folded her arms then unfolded them. She studied the pattern on the rug, grouped the lines in the ceilings by fours—did counting count as doing nothing?— she crossed her legs then uncrossed them and began to hum but stopped when Keeden shot her a look.

She inwardly groaned. She didn't find doing nothing calming at all.

He closed his eyes as if in pain. "Go away Maya."

"But—"

"Faaaaar away."

She didn't need further encouragement. She jumped up. "I'll leave you to it then."

But she didn't leave. Instead she stared at him. He looked so peaceful and being around him in this quiet space felt peaceful too. It was strange. Only this morning she'd detested this man as she had for years. But now...

Now she didn't particularly like him but she didn't *dislike* him either, which was a very odd almost disturbing feeling. As if she'd been dropped into another country where she didn't know the language or customs. She didn't know how to approach him anymore.

"You're still here," he said, his eyes still closed.

"I know."

He briefly tilted his head back. "Are you still trying to do nothing? I think you should stop. You actually lasted longer than I thought you would. I know it's a chore for you. It's hard for a lot of people so don't push yourself."

And he kept talking but she didn't listen to the words instead she listened to the deep richness of his voice...soft, soothing, engaging even encouraging. It reminded her of the ASMR artists. The ones who felt like friends, who made her feel less alone in the world.

Keeden suddenly opened his eyes, a shock of awareness coursing through her when his eyes met hers. She noticed how long his eyelashes were and remembered how once...long ago...she'd thought his eyes were beautiful.

"What is it?" he said.

"Nothing."

A quick grin touched his lips. "Are you being ironic?"

"No," Maya said, wondering why her face—no, not just her face her entire body—suddenly felt warm. Conflicting emotions flooded her. She knew she should stay away from him, but she also felt strangely drawn to him. Like a stupid month destined to get its wings singed on a bright light. It had happened before, but now in this quiet, almost tender moment, it felt as if it had never happened at all. She lowered her gaze and touched the bracelet on her wrist.

"Uh...thanks again for the jewelry." She looked at him, having gotten control of her warring emotions. "Bryant really thought I looked nice."

Keeden studied her for a moment before he nodded then turned away. "Good."

Yes, it was good. That was her goal after all.

But what wasn't good was as Maya was walking up the stairs, she wasn't remembering Bryant's big, beautiful smile, but instead Keeden's small one. It felt rare and precious.

And had affected her more than she wanted to admit.

20

———————

IT TOOK two days for the depression to hit while she worked on his project. It snuck up like a thief then pummeled her. Maya felt so depressed she couldn't eat. Even when Bryant tried to cajole her.

She needed space.

She needed hours of ASMR. But even that didn't do much to improve her mood.

She'd pictured herself helping some overestimated, over appreciated, overhyped, over *everything*, just above average black male artist with his woodblock designs and focus on getting Bryant's attention. Instead she'd been so enthralled and awed by Keeden's work she hadn't even been able to think about Bryant.

Keeden...was...great. More than great. Brilliant. He hadn't gotten lucky. He'd gone farther than she'd hoped to ever be as an artist because he was just better.

The awards, accolades, success had all been well earned.

Facing that truth was dispiriting and soul crushing. She'd hated him for years, believing he'd stolen something from her—

opportunity, resources, dreams. But he hadn't. She'd never had a chance.

Not against someone like him.

He'd also worked harder than her. She remembered more fragments of Bryant's story about him. The lean years, the struggles, the many times he could have quit but hadn't. His work hadn't reached galleries such as the Art Institute of Chicago on talent alone or just because he was a man. He'd been more driven, hustled more than she ever had. He'd done what she would have needed to if she'd wanted even half the success he'd managed to achieve.

If she could stay under the bedcovers forever she would.

Why did he have to be so skilled? It wasn't fair.

This skinny, flint eyed, bastard. How had he managed to keep a joyous, childlike spirit? His studio burst with the freedom of creativity. A freedom she'd let whither years ago.

But the absolute worst part?

He made her want to create again. She hated him for that. Hated him for whispering that she might try again, that she could do it for fun and he'd done it so carelessly.

She'd finished one of the trial woodblocks he'd begun before the accident. From the painted image clipped to one of the easels, the final print was going to be a complicated project made up of many colored woodblocks with silver and gold leaf accents forming a beautiful surreal image of a hand reaching up and grabbing a star.

Her job was to help him finish the three or four trial woodblocks for print proofs before he finalized anything. It was a time consuming project that had already taken him nine months and would likely take him the rest of the year to finish. But with her help he wouldn't have to delay it. Since most of the work had been almost completed it hadn't taken her more than six hours to finish one of them.

Using a variety of tools like chisels, knives, and awls she carefully brought forth the traced sketch he'd drawn on one of the blocks and sanded down areas, that would not be printed, until they were smooth, feeling almost at one with the wood as she inhaled its scent.

She'd then shown Keeden and he tested it by having her stain the block with paint and putting it on paper.

It was okay, but didn't get the effect he was going for, he didn't say so but she could tell by his face. So she told him not to worry and sanded some more edges down. She still didn't get the effect she wanted, didn't provide the detail that he'd sketched. She'd sanded and carved twice more until finally she lifted the block and staring back at them was the image they'd been trying to bring forward. The relief worked. There was still a lot more work to do but it was a good step forward.

Maya clapped her hands. "We did it." She turned to him, but he wasn't staring at the image he was staring at her.

"What?" Maya peered closer at the image. "Did I miss something?"

"No. You're done for the day." He motioned to the far workstation. "Go and have fun."

"Fun?"

"Yes, work on something. You can use anything you want. If it's not here let me know."

"I can't use your studio."

"Why not?"

Because I'm not a real artist, remember? You said so. "I don't have any ideas."

"The ideas come when you start working. Don't be shy, it's not like you."

It was too much. Too overwhelming. Like being asked to drive a Rolls Royce when you'd just gotten your driver's license. They weren't in the same league and she was scared.

As if sensing she was about to bolt, Keeden grabbed her arm and sat her down in front of the table. Then he put the pastels in front of her. "Use them and they're yours." He nodded at her look of surprise. "I mean it."

It was a challenge and it terrified her. Her hands shook and she gripped them in her lap. She actually had a chance to get them back. But...

But...

She took a deep breath, managed to get her hand to stop shaking and carefully opened up the case. She gazed in awe at the beautiful array of colors.

They intimidated her.

Keeden closed the case and picked it up. "If you don't want them that's fine. I already know how I'll use them." He paused, thoughtful. "I think I'll use them to create an image of a morning glory."

A flower. The jerk would use these wonderful tools to draw a flower. Not just any flower, but a deceptively alluring plant with purple flowers and curling tendrils, a creeping vine that could invade an unsuspecting garden like a coup. Left unattended, they'd cheerfully twist around anything—choking deck chairs, and prying between window eaves. She remembered her grandmother telling her how difficult they were to pull out.

No way was she going to let him draw that with *her* pastels. She held out her hand. "I'll use it."

"I've changed my mind."

She snatched them from him. "Too bad."

And what had started as a simple challenge became a door to an unexplored world. Before she knew it she was lost in creation and by the time she looked up it was dark outside.

And she was alone and she'd never felt happier. She felt like dancing, free to be herself again. He'd given her back the dream she'd lost.

But she soon realized it was all an illusion. Only people like him could afford to dream.

This wouldn't last. In less than a month she'd be back home looking for work.

She thought of crumpling the picture up but instead folded it along with any hope she'd been nurturing.

Four days later she feared she'd never manage to eat with Bryant again. She felt like such a failure, unworthy of his attention. She sat on the edge of the bed, wondering how she'd manage to finish her time there without her heart being completely broken.

21

———

"You could force her."

"How can I force her to eat?"

Keeden stared down at the untouched plate of food—a rice medley with grilled trout—Bryant had set on the kitchen counter. Keeden had suggested he take it to Maya's room, but when he had, she'd refused it.

Bryant covered the plate and put it in the fridge. "She said she's not hungry."

Keeden frowned. Maya had changed over the past several days. The first time Bryant had told him she'd cancelled dinner, Keeden hadn't taken much notice. He'd just been relieved Bryant had been willing to eat with her, which hadn't surprised him since Bryant enjoyed entertaining a captive audience (which Maya would undoubtedly be). But this was the fourth day she'd stopped eating with him. "Did you tell her I wouldn't be there?"

"Yes."

"You were clear that she'd be alone with you?"

Bryant sighed. "Yes."

"And she still turned you down?"

"Yes."

Keeden opened the fridge. "Try again. I don't think you sold it."

Bryant shook his head. "Leave it. I think she needs to be alone."

Keeden slowly closed the fridge and looked at his friend confused. "Why?"

"Your studio is something to overcome. It can be intimidating."

"I don't see why. It's nothing special."

"Only to you."

Maya had changed when he'd offer to let her use it. Maybe he shouldn't have given her back the pastels. She hadn't shown him what she'd created and he didn't ask. But something bright and alive in her had dimmed.

Had he insulted her again somehow? He'd only wanted to help. Bryant hadn't been exaggerating to say she was skilled with wood blocking, the relief she'd created had come from a steady hand. Even when he had use of his hand he hadn't gotten the effects she'd managed to. He'd thought offering her his studio would have pleased her.

Instead, she'd become polite but distant and ate her meals in her room, if she ate at all.

Perhaps it had nothing to do with him. Maybe she was overwhelmed by being with Bryant all the time. Maybe it was Bryant who intimidated her. Keeden knew how tongue-tied and nervous Maya got around his friend. It was amusing to see the transformation every time. But this was bad. She had to get over her shyness.

Her time was running out. The first week was almost over. She'd have only two more weeks to go. If she wanted to succeed with his friend, Keeden had to do something.

MAYA SQUEEZED her eyes shut and groaned when someone knocked on her bedroom door.

"I'm okay," she said in a cheery voice she used every time Bryant came to check on her.

He knocked again.

She made her voice a little louder. "I said, I'm okay."

He knocked harder. This time more insistent. Like a royal command.

She jumped up from the bed, plastered on a smile, so that her irritation wouldn't show, and swung the door open. Her mouth fell, she stared shocked. "You're not Bryant."

"No," Keeden said coming into the room. "If this is part of your plan to win him over it's not working. Let's try Plan B, shall we?"

"It's not and I don't have a Plan B."

"How about Plan G, then?"

She folded her arms. "I'm not in the mood for this."

"Let me see your work."

She laughed bitterly. "I'd never show you my work again. Not after..." She didn't finish. She didn't need to and he didn't ask her to.

"Show it to Bryant then."

"No."

"Why not? He's very exuberant. He'd make a child feel like Jacob Lawrence."

"Are you saying my work is childish?"

Keeden softly swore and looked so embarrassed she almost laughed. He didn't get embarrassed easily and almost looked cute. "No. That's not..." He sighed. "What I'm trying to say is he's safe." He bit his lip. "Unlike me."

"Right, a brutal, harsh critic."

"Maya—"

"But it's just what I need," she interrupted, coming to a decision. "I need it so that I'll stop thinking I could ever..." She abruptly turned, retrieved the picture from her drawer and handed it to him.

Keeden visibly bristled and held the paper as if she'd handed him used tissue paper. "You *folded* it up?" He shook his head. "And you call me cruel." He gently opened up the paper and rested it on the bed. He stared down at the image. "You poor thing," he said to the paper.

"It's not any good."

He studied it for a long moment before he said, "No."

She folded her arms again, tighter. "I knew it."

"But it's not bad either. You're just out of practice is all. The next attempt will be better."

"Next attempt?"

"But you know better than to fold..." Keeden briefly closed his eyes and took a deep breath before he pinned her with a glare. "Don't do that again."

Maya sat down on the bed and pointed to a section of the image, surprised he was treating her work with any respect. "But this part is out of proportion and this space didn't come out the way I'd wanted it to. It's terrible."

"It's not terrible."

"You said it wasn't good."

"Right and we both know I'd be lying if I said it was, but I didn't say it was terrible. You've got skills. You know that. But even more important, you love doing it."

She lowered her gaze, feeling as if he'd exposed a secret part of her. "How do you know that?"

"You looked happy while you were working on it."

She looked up at him surprised. "You were watching me?"

Keeden looked embarrassed again, but this time, instead of

looking mildly cute, he looked adorable. Which was weird because Keeden was far from adorable.

But his flustered look made her look at him in a new way. He didn't seem as distant and austere as usual. She didn't see a snake, she saw a man. "No, I just...you were in the studio so long I assumed." He cleared his throat. "Anyway, a studio and pastels needs to be used and since I'm out of commission for the time being," he waved his cast, "you should use it." He walked to the door. "Also, Bryant's been asking about you. Stop eating in your room."

He left before she could reply.

22

———

THE SNAKE MUST HAVE PUT her under a spell because, first, Maya could no longer see him as a snake anymore. She saw Keeden. An irritating, at times frustrating, strangely funny Keeden, but Keeden all the same.

And two, although she stopped eating in her room, instead of eating with Bryant (as she had planned and dreamed of doing) she ended up eating with Keeden.

And the spell remained strong because it didn't bother her at all.

The first time they'd ended up eating together had been a mistake.

One night she'd worked later than usual, one of the wood blocking tools hadn't been behaving the way she'd wanted it to and that had her running late. She texted Bryant to start dinner without her and then finished. After that, she had an idea she wanted to try with the pastels and somehow two hours passed before a figure shadowed her work. She looked up and saw Keeden. She quickly covered her work.

"I'm not here to judge," he said.

"Then what do you want?"

"You haven't stopped. You need to eat something." He shook his head when she opened her mouth. "This is not a suggestion. Come on."

He led her to the kitchen and a covered plate. "Enjoy."

She sat at the kitchen island. "Have you eaten yet?" she said and smiled when he hesitated. "It's a simple question."

"I'm about to start."

She looked around the kitchen. "Where's your food?"

He gestured vaguely towards another room.

"You'll have to be more specific than that."

"The living room."

"Which one. I know you have two." She grabbed a tray. "Never mind just lead the way."

He looked at her alarmed. "What are you doing?"

"I'm going to eat with you." She paused amused by the startled look on his face. "Unless...the sight of me gives you indigestion. The possibility has been brought up before."

"No, it's just...I watch a show while I eat."

"I guessed as much. I didn't think you'd sit in the living room and stare at the wall. Then again you do like to do nothing."

He bit his lip.

"It's okay, if I don't like the show I'll leave. I won't judge."

"Yes you will," he mumbled then walked to the living room where he had his food laid out on a standing tray.

She walked past him and sat down. Within minutes she saw why he'd hesitated to invite her.

"You like to watch surgical shows while you're eating?"

He kept his gaze fixed on the large flat screen. "I like animals."

"On operating tables."

"I like seeing their lives getting saved."

Fortunately, she didn't have a queasy stomach and she too started to worry about the dog that had been attacked by a porcupine. "I hope they'll get all the quills out."

"She will," Keeden said referring to the popular vet. "She's very meticulous as are her assistants. Hopefully, this time, he'll learn his lesson."

"This time?"

He nodded. "Yes, this is his second trip to the vet for the same injury."

Maya laughed and Keeden flashed one of his rare smiles and told her about a dog who'd gotten attacked by a skunk four times.

After that, eating together and watching a veterinary show became routine. Neither arranged it that way it just sort of happened. She'd work on one of his projects and then spend time working on something just for herself and then he'd tell her it was time to stop and she'd find food waiting for her and a space on the couch beside him.

"Does Bryant ever watch these shows?" she'd asked him the second night as they cleared the dishes.

"You should ask him."

"I'm asking you."

"No, seriously," Keeden said amused. "You should ask him and see his face. It's worth the effort."

So she did the next day, in the studio after he'd finished discussing an upcoming project with Keeden.

"D-do you watch *Amazing Vets*?" she asked him as he headed to the door.

Bryant slowly turned and shot Keeden a look. "Did you tell her?"

Keeden held up his hands in surrender. "Not a word. I promised."

Bryant took a step towards where she sat behind her workstation. "This evil man had me watch an episode where they worked on this poor dog for hours and then it *died*."

Keeden shook his head. "I didn't know it was going to die."

"I'll never watch it again. Never. It's too sad."

"Y-you should give it…um…another chance," Maya said. "It's not sad. There are lots of happy stories."

His brows shot up. "He's got you watching it too?"

His surprise caused her to hesitate. She thought of denying it, knowing that she'd lose some points in his eyes, but she didn't want to pretend either. "Yes. I don't mind it." An understatement but not a complete lie.

Bryant sniffed. "At least you don't watch it while eating like this sicko does."

Maya didn't know what gave her away, but Bryant's eyebrows rose even higher. "You must be joking. You can watch all that gore while eating? What is wrong with you?"

"He's a bad influence," Maya said. "I'm trying to recover."

Bryant shook his head and left.

Maya buried her face in her hands. "I think I just ruined my chances."

"Look on the bright side."

She let her hands fall to the table and looked at Keeden, doubtful. "Bright side?"

"You were able to talk to him using full sentences."

She straightened. That was true. Her heart hadn't pounded nearly as hard as it usually did. She hadn't felt out of breath. She'd actually managed to talk to him about something.

That made him sick.

She buried her face in her hands again and groaned. "It's over."

"No, he'll find you even more interesting now. He'll try to reconcile that sweet face of yours with enjoying gore."

"It's not as if we're watching a slaughterhouse." She

paused. She narrowed her eyes at him. "Wait...did he say I had a sweet face?"

A strange expression crossed Keeden's face before he nodded and said, "Yeah, sure. He's said that."

"No one's ever called me sweet looking before. Especially compared to my sisters. Ava's the sweet one."

"Which one are you?"

Maya opened her mouth then closed it. She shook her head. "You already know. You've been hearing it for years."

"What I've heard may not be what you've heard," Keeden said.

"What have you heard?"

"You first."

"No, I don't want to talk about it." It was too painful to do so. To be reminded she was the short one (she was too stocky to be considered petite), the other one, the screw up and if anyone mentioned her features they said she was "pretty enough" like a knock-off piece of furniture someone settled for when they couldn't afford the real thing.

To her relief Keeden fell silent then said, "It was worth asking him though, wasn't it?"

She remembered the horror on Bryant's face and instead of feeling mortified she laughed. "You are an evil man."

"Careful, I might rub off on you."

"I doubt that."

"Why?"

She grinned. "Because I can be a little evil myself."

Keeden didn't grin back, instead a devilish look entered his eyes and he slowly blinked, as if sending her a silent daring message that said "I'd like to see you try."

Her heart skipped a beat because she wanted to take up that challenge and offer one of her own and that's when she knew she wasn't only a little evil, she'd gone a little crazy too.

That night she buried her face in her pillow and tried to think of how to redouble her efforts.

Bryant. The only reason she was here in Keeden's house was because of Bryant.

She took a deep, calming breath and tried to conjure up his beautiful image in her mind.

Yes, there. She basked in the memory of his warm eyes and smile. He'd said she had a sweet face. She pressed her face to her hands, feeling a happy glow. He always made her feel so wonderful.

He was definitely the man for her, but the clock was ticking. Keeden had given her three weeks. One week was already gone and although Keeden didn't seem in a hurry to get rid of her, she wouldn't push her luck.

The following morning Maya dressed with extra care thinking of the different things she'd ask Bryant. She would even try to eat dinner with him. He was patient with her halting attempts and she had to practice if she wanted to become a charming conversationalist and finally win him over.

She met him in the kitchen and he apologized for being in a rush then handed her a manila envelope and asked her to give it to Keeden.

Keeden wasn't in his studio or the informal living room so the third place she looked was his study. The door stood ajar and she heard angry mumbling.

She knocked, pushed the door wider and stepped inside only to face a headless monster.

23

———

A green headless monster.

A fiercely swearing green headless monster.

"What are you doing?"

The monster froze. "What do you think I'm doing?"

The stubborn man was trying to put on a long sleeve shirt but hadn't managed to get it over his cast or his head.

She walked into the room. She'd learned that this wood paneled space with the chrome desk and laptop was where Keeden conducted business since he didn't let outsiders into his studio. "Let me help you."

"No."

"Stay still." Before he could argue she pulled the shirt off. "Better."

He glared at her. "I was trying to put it *on* not take it off."

"It's too tight and it won't fit over the cast. Why are you trying to put something over your head anyway? You should try a button down shirt."

"No, the cast won't fit that either. I need to look formal."

"We could cut it—"

"I'm not cutting my clothes."

"You can buy another—"

"No."

"Fine, then put on a T-shirt. Or a Ghanaian smock. Why get dressed up anyway?"

Keeden gestured to the laptop with his left hand. "I have a videoconference in ten minutes."

"Ten minutes?"

"Glad your hearing is still up to snuff."

"Why did you wait so late?"

"I didn't think it'd take this long..." He released a sound of frustration. "Doesn't matter. Leave me alone. You're wasting precious time."

Maya ignored him. "You can't wear that." She glanced around the room then stopped at a folded piece of cloth resting on one of the chairs.

His gaze followed hers. "No."

"Yes, this is perfect." She pounced on it. "The pattern is gorgeous. Your stepmother chose it, right?"

"I'm not—"

"Just stand still."

"No, I'm not wearing a sash."

"I won't make it look like that. Trust me."

"Trusting you is against my nature. Why would I do that?"

"Because I'm your only choice not to go shirtless on this video call."

Keeden glanced at the clock and swore.

"That doesn't sound very polite," Maya said with faux offense.

He met her gaze without a shred of humor. "This is me being polite." He frowned at the cloth in her hand. "Get on with it then."

"Thank you. This won't take long and I promise I'll make

you look presentable." When it came to headscarves and her own hair she was a disaster, but give her a piece of cloth for clothes and suddenly she was a pro, especially for other people.

Maya began expertly fashioning the cloth around his torso like a loose shirt. It was strange being this close to him. She didn't expect to notice how nice he smelled (like fresh mint and sweetened coconut) or that he wasn't as skinny as she'd always imagined him to be. He had muscle definition. Nothing like Bryant's big, tall frame of course, but he had nice shoulders and his arms were like corded steel. Then she noticed the bruises on his chest and felt a twinge of guilt. They looked painful.

"You stopped," Keeden said. "What is it?"

"You don't heal very fast, do you? You have so many bruises." She clicked her tongue in pity. "Did you get hit by a car or something?"

She met his gaze. Icicles shot back.

"Not funny?" she said.

"Laughing hurts."

"Still?"

"Yes."

She bit her lip. "Oh, sorry."

Keeden narrowed his eyes. "I seriously doubt that."

Maya stepped back and studied her handiwork. The transformation surprised her. He looked like a tribal prince. While western clothing seemed to emphasize his slender build the cloth emphasized the richness of his brown skin, the proud stance of his body, the beautiful long, black hair, the width of his shoulders—he looked strong, in control, powerful.

He almost looked...handsome. Which was impossible. She took another step back and bowed her head in mock modesty. "You're all set, sah, with two minutes to spare."

And acting as if he truly was a prince and she a lowly seamstress Keeden sat behind his desk, turned on the laptop and studied his image reflected on the screen. He gave one curt nod, a sign he was pleased, then dismissed her with a wave of his hand.

She pulled a face.

He ignored her.

But he still managed to make her smile.

24

———

HE HAD TO FIND HER.

After his videoconference Keeden immediately went to his studio to see if Maya was there.

He didn't want to see her to tell her that the conference went well. That more than one person complimented him on his shirt or that he'd barely remembered what he'd said because all he could think about was the mango tinged scent of her lotion. The brush of her hair under his chin.

He didn't want to see her to say anything or even do anything, he just wanted to see her because seeing her made him happy.

But Maya wasn't in the studio.

Keeden pushed down his disappointment and checked the clock. Oh, that's right, he'd forgotten. Maya should be in the kitchen taking a break with Bryant right now.

He was only partially right. Bryant was in the kitchen.

His friend gave him the once over then produced a low whistle of appreciation.

"Shut up." Keeden looked around. "Where's Maya?"

"Said she had to run an errand but she'd be right back."

He tamped down another wave of disappointment.

"You look good. I've never seen that style before. Where did you get that?"

"Maya made it up."

Bryant furrowed his brows. "Made it up?"

"Took a piece of cloth and fashioned it this way."

Bryant circled him, impressed. "This is from one piece of cloth?"

"Yes, so don't tug at it."

Bryant snatched his hand back. "Amazing."

His chef, Louisa Nyugen, a woman in her sixties with purple highlights in her short black hair, could chop with such speed a knife seemed to become invisible. She walked into the kitchen with her typical confident stride then halted and whistled at him.

Keeden frowned. "Stop with the whistling."

"You look good."

"It's Maya's doing," Bryant told her.

"No surprise," she said.

Bryant nodded. "She should help you more often."

"It's only because of the cast," Keeden said. "I know how to dress."

They shared a look.

"What?"

"You tell him," Louisa said, pulling out a skillet. "Job security is important to me."

"You don't like how I dress?" Keeden said.

Bryant folded his arms. "For a guy who's an artist you dress with the flair of a funeral director."

"No, I don't."

"Is there any color in your wardrobe?" He pointed at him. "Besides white, black and grey."

"White, black and grey are colors," he mumbled.

"You put all your focus on your work and go around looking scary instead of stylish."

"Scary?"

"You look like the kind of guy who'd keep a vile of blood in your coat pocket," Louisa said, adding chopped vegetables to the now heated skillet and a spice that scented the air with black pepper.

"Are you comparing me to a vampire?"

"Without the fangs."

"What was that comment about job security," Keeden said in a dry voice.

Louisa moved the vegetables around in the skillet and shrugged. "I realized no one else would be willing to put up with you."

"I do not dress like a vampire."

"Not that the vampire look isn't sexy," Bryant said before Louisa could argue, "it's just intimidating and you could consider softening your appearance. It's just a suggestion."

"Oh, there you are," his housekeeper, Mathilde Faron said before he could reply. She'd only been working for him for the past five years but it felt longer. She managed to accept his eccentric habits—visitors were only allowed in three locations; he liked staff kept out of his way (preferably he didn't like to see them at all); and never bother him when he's in his studio unless there's a fire. She was as commanding as a general with a broad build and circular glasses that seemed to permanently sit on the edge of her nose.

She stopped in the entryway when he turned. She pushed her glasses to the bridge of her nose and looked him up and down.

He pointed at her. "Whistle and you're fired."

She bit her lip.

"Why were you looking for me?"

"You'd better get in the bath before it gets cold," she said.

"Bath?"

"Yes, I just saw Maya and she said she has one ready for you. She timed it so that it'd be ready by the end of your meeting."

"How did she know when my meeting would end?"

"The same way we all know your schedule," Mathilde said pulling out her cell phone. "Your VA."

His virtual assistant helped to keep him organized but it was a little unsettling to have so many people know his business. What was more annoying was he was seeing everyone else but the one person he'd wanted to.

Then another thought struck him. If she'd prepared a bath for him that meant... "She's been in my room?"

"No, she prepared the second bath not the one for the master bedroom. She told me to mention that."

Keeden felt his mild panic ebb, slightly. She'd said she wouldn't go into his bedroom and she'd kept her word. "I don't want or need a bath."

"Yes, you do."

"It'll be relaxing," Louisa said, covering the vegetables before heading for the fridge.

"That's why she's not here," Bryant said. "She bought bath salts to aid in healing your bruises."

"Just do it," Mathilde said.

"No."

Bryant reached forward to tug on the makeshift shirt. "If you need help—"

Keeden jumped away from him. "I'm fine. Where is she?"

"Instead of searching for her, just take the bath. You'll see her later."

Bryant started to grin. A dangerous grin that Keeden hated.

A grin that meant his friend saw something Keeden didn't want him to. "Unless you're missing her so much—"

"I'll take the damn bath," he lied because it was easier than admitting Bryant was right or taking a plate and throwing it at him.

Keeden left the kitchen. He wasn't taking a bath. He hadn't indulged in one since he was... what? Nine? Who had the time? Or inclination? And why would Maya think he needed one? He'd taken a shower that morning so he knew he didn't smell, and he felt his bruises were healing nicely, even if he was still a little sore when he did certain movements.

Keeden marched to the bath ready to empty it out. Then stopped at the lavender scented air, the soft tendrils of steam touching his skin, the lit candles. He didn't need candles or the pillow or the damn... Did she actually leave him a note?

He picked it up and read, "I know your videoconference went well because I made you look so good. Now you can relax."

Her arrogance made him smile. He set the note down. Seeing her would have been better than a note, but...

He'd hate to waste all this water and it was warm and his body still did ache. What the hell?

He stripped down, swept his hair up then sank into the warm water with a contended sigh. Heaven.

He lifted the note, studied the loops of her letters, the little smiley face she'd drawn in the corner and felt another smile form and then...

Then...

He came to his senses.

They hit him like an anvil.

He crumpled the note in his fist as anger mingled with longing. Why was she doing this to him? Why was she taking care of him? Making him feel this way? Was she getting him out of the way so she could be with Bryant? That didn't make sense. She didn't need a reason.

Why had he gone searching for her in the first place? *Unless you're missing her so much...* Bryant had teased him. This time his friend's harmless teasing hadn't annoyed him. It had stung.

He was chasing shadows.

And now no matter how much he knew—he knew!!—he still had a stupid, irrational desire to see her, now...no, it was worse. Now he didn't only want to see her.

He wanted her to join him.

He wanted her to walk through the bathroom door, strip down until every blessed inch of her luscious brown body was visible and sink into the water with him. He wanted to feel her body wrap around him as the single piece of cloth had.

Keeden briefly rested his head back on the pillow and swore. That wasn't like him. He didn't usually have thoughts like that. She was making a fool of him again.

Why did she constantly have to surprise him?

He had looked better in the newly fashioned garment she'd made for him. Even more, he felt better. The material worked. He usually stayed away from too many patterns (or any patterns at all), he didn't want to overemphasize his cultural and ethnic background as a number of other artists did, cleverly making their origin part of their brand identity.

He wasn't a showy artist. He liked being invisible behind his work. But maybe he didn't need to be so invisible. Perhaps a little color would be good for his image. He'd also found himself thinking in new interesting ways, feeling like a different person as if he didn't have to be stuck as the artist he'd been for years. His future didn't have to mirror his past. He felt a new Keeden emerging.

His stepmother and sister were always telling him about

the tailor they worked with but Keeden didn't like the man's designs. But maybe Maya could help.

Maya.

He liked her. How that had happened he didn't want to think about, but it was a fact he couldn't deny.

He also found her attractive.

Very attractive.

That was fine too. Bryant had casually mentioned Maya's looks on numerous occasions but Keeden refused to believe it was true. But now he could see the appeal of her soft round figure, her temptingly full lips, her sharp brown eyes. But his wayward thoughts were simple flights of fancy nothing more—they couldn't be more. It was only because he'd never known her like this and the bath and the success of his videoconference had lifted his mood.

That was all. Nothing else.

Keeden left the bathroom feeling more in control. He changed into a T-shirt before he headed downstairs.

He met Bryant on his way to the studio. "I'd like to talk to you Friday about—"

"Sorry, can we make it next week?" Bryant said. "I'm taking Maya to a concert."

Keeden could only nod, feeling as if he'd been punched in the gut.

25

—————

"If you want to come along—"

"No," Keeden said quickly, trying his best not to feel sick. Why did he feel sick? There was no reason to. "That's okay. You need a break. Enjoy yourselves."

He turned before Bryant could say anything else and headed for his studio as if on autopilot.

His body moved but he wasn't in complete control of it. All the relaxed tension and ease he'd felt only moments before slowly drained away with each step, like the water in the now empty tub.

Bryant had a date with Maya.

Maya was going out with Bryant.

She'd achieved her goal.

She was in his house because of Bryant.

Not him.

Maya hadn't agreed to the elders' plan because she'd wanted to help him but because she wanted a chance to get closer to his best friend.

He couldn't forget that.

That silly string bean? Isn't he funny?

Maya's taunting words from all those years ago, swirled in his mind, twisting his heart. Funny indeed.

Keeden mindlessly walked into the studio and saw Maya cleaning up. That was a good thing. She'd clean up and leave.

Then he'd be alone.

He needed to be alone.

She looked over at him and smiled.

And that's when Keeden knew he was doomed. He couldn't hate her anymore. He couldn't stay away either.

He couldn't seem to control his growing feelings for her. Even though he knew she could hurt him. He knew he should keep his distance. In spite of all that, he didn't want her to go. He wanted her to stay until his cast came off.

After that there'd be nothing holding her there, but he'd come up with something. Make up another project. Hire her. He'd figure something out.

He didn't want to lose her to Bryant.

He respected his friend but really knew that Maya wasn't his type. Or was that wishful thinking?

Even if Bryant's type had changed and Maya truly got Bryant to fall for her.

Keeden didn't want to lose her.

He wanted her in his life. He wanted her as a friend.

Not a nemesis.

That silly string bean? Isn't he funny?

Keeden felt a soft hand on his arm and the sweetened scent of mangoes briefly embraced him, as a tender hand touched his neck.

"You're not warm," Maya mumbled, pulling his arm. "Come on sit down."

He blinked and glanced down at her. "What?"

She led him to the small couch behind the coffee table

where he and Bryant sat when they were coming up with ideas or when he wanted to take a nap. She gently pushed him down. "I asked did you enjoy your bath and you stood there like a statue. Are you feeling okay?"

"Hmm." He glanced up at the sculpture hanging from the ceiling, his heart beating too fast at the sight of her smile.

Maya folded her arms and clicked her tongue. "Is that the thanks I get?"

"You didn't have to do it."

She playfully patted his cheek. "There you go again stating the obvious."

If she was anybody else he would have been annoyed but instead he was just glad she noticed him.

He had to keep his distance, he had to keep his cool. It was the only way to protect himself. He stiffened. "Hmm."

"I went too far, didn't I?" she said, her voice holding a note of regret. "I overstepped my bounds and made you angry."

Keeden looked at her sad eyes and quickly said, "No," with a ferocity that surprised them both. But he wouldn't make her cry again. He sighed and attempted to soften his tone. "No. I'm just not used to—"

"Me being nice?" Maya guessed with a laugh. "Me neither. But after seeing..." She rubbed her hands together, sent a pointed look at his chest then his cast. "I'm truly sorry about what happened to you."

He shook his head. "We've gotten past that."

"I still needed to say it. And the funeral flowers really were a mistake."

"I know." He still remembered the shocked look on her face from that day. But he'd done nothing to help her. He'd let her take the blame.

And yet here she was apologizing to him. As if she cared. "You don't have to pretend," he said in a cold voice.

"Pretend?"

"To care about me."

"I'm not pretending," she shot back. "I do care. Don't ask me why because I don't know. Especially when you turn on me like this and treat me like..." She gripped her hands into fists. "I'm so beneath you you can barely look at me."

Keeden jumped to his feet, alarmed by the tears in her voice. "I'm embarrassed." He nodded at her surprised expression. "Really." He bit his lip. "I'm...glad you care." *Even though it hurts. Even though seeing your eyes soften and a gentle look of relief spread over your face tugs at my heart.* He cleared his throat desperate to change the subject. "I...heard you have a date."

Maya frowned. "A date?"

Keeden swallowed. Did she really need him to spell it out? "With Bryant."

She laughed. "A date? No, it's nothing like that. Bryant and I are going to an outdoor concert this Friday that's all."

"Sounds like a date to me."

"Thanks, but it's not really. He got tickets from a friend he didn't want to go to waste."

Keeden silently swore. He couldn't believe his friend was still using that lie. It was a handy one he used when he didn't want to officially ask someone out. One thing was certain, his friend was curious about her. He didn't spring that story on anyone he wasn't interested in. "Hmm." Keeden gestured to the door. "You should go. I didn't mean to keep you."

"You're not."

She should be leaving. Why wasn't she leaving? Why was she looking at him as if she planned to stay?

He sat back down and stared down at the table. "What you did today, think you could do it again?"

"You want another bath?" Maya said confused.

Keeden sent her a sideward glance. "No...I mean the uh shirt."

"Your stepmother's tailor could—"

"No," he said with a little too much force. He softened his voice, he didn't want to scare her. "I don't want the typical. It doesn't work."

She nodded and studied him for a long moment. "You're right. You usually end up looking as skinny as a flagpole."

"Can you help or not?"

"I've got some ideas and you can use my tailor. Like you, there are certain outfits I can't just take off the rack, especially dresses. I know I'm short and stocky and can look ridiculous in gowns. I once tried one on with a V-neck so deep it literally plunged to my belly button. Fortunately, my tailor's very skilled and with a couple well-placed stitches, made me look beautiful."

"So, basically he's a miracle worker."

"Yes," Maya said recognizing the insult. "He might actually make you look *tall*."

Keeden nodded impressed by her biting retort. "Good. I just need two or three items. I'll pay you."

"Okay."

"You can use the extra cloth that's left over for yourself."

Maya laughed. "There wouldn't be enough cloth to fit me."

"She gave me three stacks."

"You don't go by the stack you go by the yard."

"I have enough cloth to cover a car."

Maya folded her arms. "Oh thanks."

"I didn't mean—"

"I know." She let her arms fall. "Look, if there's cloth left over fine. I'll take it. Even if it's only enough to make a bra."

Keeden looked suddenly pensive, his gaze dipping to her chest. "You're right. There might not be—" He stopped.

She stared at him. "Go on."

"No. Go away."

"It's not like you to stop mid-insult."

"It wasn't an insult."

"It wasn't going to be a compliment."

"How do you know that?"

"Because we're talking about you. I think if you complimented me your tongue would shrivel up and fall out of your mouth."

He paused. Let his gaze slide over her figure before he said, "I think you have great attributes. How's that for a compliment?" he said in a teasing velvet tone.

She stared at him stunned.

"Amazing. My tongue's still working." He stood and walked to the door.

"Where are you going?"

"I'm getting a snack," he said in a tone that said "Leave me alone."

A tone he knew she'd ignore.

He didn't look back when she followed him and tried his best to hide a smile.

26

———

"So how did it happen?" Keeden asked once they were in the kitchen.

"What?" Maya asked, popping a grape in her mouth. They sat at the kitchen island: She eating grapes and cheese and he roasted chickpeas.

"The date."

She ate another grape and frowned. "I told you it's not a date."

"Well, it's not a business meeting."

"You could come along if you want. He even suggested it."

Keeden scratched the tip of his nose and flashed a sour grin. "Relax, I turned him down."

Maya nodded surprised to feel disappointed. Even more surprised that she didn't want to talk about it. She should feel victorious.

Only weeks ago news like this would have sent her over the moon, but now she felt mildly...unsatisfied. Bryant saw her as a friend but the strange thing was she was starting to see him the same way. He was still amazing, beautiful to look at, but just a guy. Instead she kept thinking about how Keeden had complimented her.

In a low silky tone that had made her inwardly shiver in delight.

She remembered how he'd softened his cold tone and confessed that he'd been embarrassed about her caring about him. Why would he feel embarrassed? She'd expected him to say 'annoyed' or 'irritated' that he found her a busybody. Instead he looked a little shy and vulnerable. She'd seen hints of awkward moments before but nothing like that. She wanted to know more about him. So much more. What was happening to her?

Keeden nudged her with his elbow. "I said relax."

She turned to him. "Relax?"

"Yes, you suddenly got this horrified look on your face. You don't have to worry, I'm not coming. You can keep your dear Bryant all to yourself."

"Right." Bryant. She was supposed to think about him. "There's your proof. He was willing for you to tag along so it's not a date."

"You could turn it into one."

"He asked me to go with him because he thought I needed a break from you. He thinks that I've been working hard without a break these past weeks."

"I give you breaks. You're the one who doesn't take them. Did you tell him that? Of course not because I have to be the villain."

"No one sees you as the villain. But you aren't the easiest person to work with."

"Yes, I am." He stared at her surprised. "Do you really need a break from me?"

No. "Absolutely." But not in the way that either man thought she did. She'd been thinking of Keeden way too much and the thought of leaving after her three weeks were up made her heart sink. She'd tried to come up with reasons to stay a little longer. But she'd never let him know that. "You can be a nuisance."

"A nuisance?"

She nodded. "Who can listen to the entire soundtrack of *Cowboy Bebop* five hundred times?"

Keeden took a long swallow of his grape juice then glanced at her in a way that was oddly sexy. He sent her a secretive look as if he knew something she didn't.

"You find that annoying huh?" he said.

"Of course."

"How did you know the music was from *Cowboy Bebop*?"

Maya paused. Her mind went blank. She was caught. She couldn't admit that she knew about that classic anime series. No more than she'd admit that she didn't mind the lo-fi hip hop beats of *Samuari Champloo* that he also liked to listen to. No self-respecting grown woman would admit to knowing the soundtrack to an animation series. She might as well admit to knowing the entire soundtrack to *The Little Mermaid* as well.

Keeden continued to study her. "Well?"

"I saw the name."

He shook his head. "No, you didn't."

"A cousin of mine liked the show."

"Which cousin?"

"You wouldn't know them."

"Try again."

She snapped her fingers as if a thought had just occurred to her. "I know. It was an art class. The artwork for the anime is gorgeous. I saw one episode for research purposes."

"Research?"

"Yes."

Keeden grinned. "You're a terrible liar."

She didn't care. She would admit to nothing.

He shrugged. "All right I'll try some other songs too."

"Thank you."

"*Aladdin* maybe?"

"Shut up."

He began to sing "A Whole New World."

"You're obnoxious."

He affected a terrible Caribbean accent and began singing "Under the Sea."

Maya giggled. "Stop it." She pointed at him. "How do you know the lyrics?"

"Lena couldn't get enough of it. I also know 'What's This?'"

"From the *Nightmare Before Christmas?*"

"Exactly."

She laughed.

He grinned and her heart did something it should never have done. No, this was Keeden. He was not supposed to affect her this way. Make her blood boil, yes, but make her heart race? Absolutely not.

He'd never made her feel nervous before. She'd never noticed how big and long fingered his hands were. She was used to people being taller than her, but sitting next to him like this with her feet barely reaching the foot wrung, it felt even more obvious how much more of him there was than her.

She'd never been so aware of him before.

And she didn't want their time to end yet.

She took a deep breath. "Um...I was wondering."

He scratched his nose. "I'd like to ask you something."

"You first," they both said.

"No, you," they said again.

Maya released a nervous laugh and Keeden briefly hung his head before he motioned to her.

And she lost the courage. She didn't want to hear him say no. She had another week. She didn't want to jeopardize that.

He poked her. "I'm brilliant but I've yet to gain the ability to read minds."

"It's okay. I changed my mind."

He nodded.

They fell silent.

"I want an extension," she said in a rush.

"I think you should stay longer," he said.

"What?" they chorused.

She blinked at him. "You want me to stay longer?"

He gaped back at her. "You want to stay longer?"

"Yes...I like working here and until you get your cast off I think it was selfish of me to only give you three weeks."

"Right."

"When does the cast come off?"

"Another four weeks."

"Oh." She bit her lip. "So you like me helping you?"

"No, but I enjoy torturing myself by keeping you around."

Maya folded her arms on the island, rested her head down and groaned.

"What?"

She straightened and said in a grim voice, "I guess we have to admit it."

"Admit what?"

"We're friends now."

Keeden feigned a look of such abject horror Maya couldn't help but laugh.

He rested a hand on his chest. "Do we have to go that far?"

"Yes."

"But f-friends?"

"Yes," she repeated with a feeling of certainty. "I actually like you."

He took a handful of chickpeas and silently munched on them.

"This is where you agree."

"Agree to what?"

"Keeden."

He rolled his eyes. "Do I have to say it?"

She picked up a grape and rolled it between her thumb and forefinger. "Maybe I shouldn't extend my stay. Bryant—"

Keeden snatched the grape from her and popped it in his mouth. "Fine. I admit the feeling is unfortunately mutual."

Maya smiled relieved.

He studied her for a minute. "You didn't really doubt it, did you?"

"When it comes to you, I take nothing for granted."

He nodded. "Wise choice."

"You could wake up tomorrow morning and hate me all over again."

He glanced down at the chickpeas and mumbled, "I wish I could."

"What?"

"Never mind."

"Good. We're friends now." She pressed a finger to her lips. "But nobody needs to know yet."

He looked at her and sniffed. "They wouldn't believe us anyway."

"I can hardly believe it myself."

"Me too." He held her gaze then turned away. "So that's settled." He stood. "Enjoy your date."

She grabbed one of his braids and tugged it. "It's not a date."

He spun around and stared at her stunned before he pulled his hair over his shoulder and checked for damages. "I think you're too violent to be friends with."

"A man with hair as long as yours shouldn't annoy me."

Keeden pushed his hair back and let his hair swing. "Careful you sound jealous."

Maya rubbed her hands together and mimicked the voice of the crackling Wicked Witch of the West from *The Wizard of Oz*. "Scissors I need. I need scissors."

To her surprise Keeden threw his head back and laughed. A rich warm sound that made her stare at him and realize she didn't just like him. She liked him a lot.

She frowned and folded her arms. "You really are a nuisance. You're supposed to be trembling in fear not laughing."

"I'd no sooner tremble at the sight of a chipmunk. But I need a favor."

"You just compared me to a chipmunk and you're asking for a favor?"

"It's an improvement on a rat, right?"

"Right now you're shoveling yourself into quicksand."

He turned. "Forget it."

She was too curious to let him leave. "What is it?"

He slowly turned back to her with a smug grin. "I'm not sure you'll be up to it."

She folded her arms eager for a challenge. "Try me."

27

———————

HE WANTED her to wash his hair. His beautiful hair.

It was like asking her to carry a beloved fragile heirloom on a tray while crossing a tightrope strung between two twenty-story buildings.

It was a big favor to ask. Hair wash day was usually an all day affair especially with hair the length of his.

"Don't you go to a salon?"

"No."

"You wash your *own* hair?"

"Yes." Keeden lowered his voice to a conspiratorial whisper. "Millions do."

Maya patted her chest. "You'd actually trust me with your hair?"

"Yes. We're friends now, right?"

"Is this some sort of test?"

"No." He shrugged. "After my accident my stepmother had someone come to the house, but then he tried to seduce me—"

"What?"

"Some people find me attractive, you know."

"It's not that. It's just…bold."

"When you have money people tend to be. But if you don't think you can do it—"

"I can do it," she said, sounding more certain than she felt.

"Good. My schedule's free tomorrow. Say ten o'clock?"

"No, problem."

Of course it was a problem. She'd always wanted to get her hands on his hair. In the past she'd imagined fashioning it around his neck, but this time she knew this was a chance to seal their friendship.

He'd trusted her with his work and now he trusted her with his hair. She wouldn't fail him.

That night Maya scoured through numerous online videos about natural hair care and took notes as if she were cramming for an exam. While she wore her hair natural, the texture of Keeden's hair was different than hers—hers was thinner and like string that would float; his was thick like rope that would sink—and she didn't want to make any major errors but there was so much differing advice she ended up with a headache.

She barely slept that night but met him with a bright grin the following morning so it wouldn't show. In the casual living room she put on *Amazing Vets* while she undid his long braids, at times letting her fingers slide down the strands, reveling in their soft feel. What if she tore it, snagged it, pulled at his scalp? What was she doing? She started to section his hair into six parts.

He suddenly reached back and covered her hand with his. "It's all right, Maya."

She froze, stunned by the warmth of his palm. "What?"

"I can feel your hands shaking."

"I'm sorry." She gripped the large tooth comb. "Am I pulling your hair?"

"No, you're shaking and breathing like you're on the verge of suffocation."

She laughed then sighed. "I'm nervous."

"Wouldn't have guessed." He removed his hand. "Just do your best. My choices were you or Bryant and I chose you."

Somehow that made her feel better. He'd chosen her. He trusted her. She could do this.

She finished sectioning his hair then took him to the bathroom where there was a shower hose.

They decided to use the bathtub, kneeling over the side, since his hair was so long and it'd be awkward at the sink (and there was no way she was getting in the shower with him).

She released one of the sections of hair and turned on the faucet and all her fears melted away as the water rushed over it.

Rivers of water made the attractive zig zag pattern of his natural thick black hair become more pronounced. Her emotions swung from awe to envy. It wasn't fair. Her hair barely reached her shoulders and when it got wet plastered to her head like a carpet.

"Are you trying to drown me now?"

"Oh, sorry," Maya said redirecting the spray. "You've got beautiful hair."

"You've only just noticed?"

She sprayed his face.

He swore and sputtered.

"My wrist slipped," she said.

"You're an evil woman."

"You shouldn't insult me when you're in such a vulnerable position."

"Hmm."

Even the shampoo he used seemed to be a luxury item: cool cucumber scented with a touch of mint. She finished washing his hair then grabbed a towel to help him dry it. He slapped her hand away and picked up the old T-shirt he'd brought with him and wrapped it around his head. Keeden looked at her horrified. "Why would you do that?"

"What?"

"Use a towel?"

Maya looked at him confused. "I always use a towel to dry my hair."

Keeden looked pained for a moment. "Well, you shouldn't. Towels tend to pull our hair. You need a smooth surface material." He tried awkwardly to dry his hair.

"Let me help you. That's why I'm here."

"I didn't mean to be brusque."

"It's okay, I've gotten used to it." But she was glad for the apology all the same. She felt like an idiot. All this time she didn't know you weren't suppose to towel your hair dry. Her mother and sisters did it all the time. "All done."

He cleared his throat and an expression crossed his face she was beginning to recognize: embarrassment. "I use a deep conditioner."

She snapped her fingers. "Oh right of course. Leave-in or rinse out?"

"Usually rinse out but—"

"It's okay, I don't mind." Plus she was curious to find out what he used.

His deep moisturizing conditioner smelled heavenly. She probably put too much product in his hair but she had so much fun running her fingers through it she couldn't help herself. Maya then twisted his hair into four large sections and wrapped it in a silk wrap to let the conditioner do its job. She didn't remember how they ended up ordering pizza and watching *Cowboy Bebop* for nearly two hours. Afterwards she rinsed his hair and moisturized it again with a moisture spray and Shea butter and put it into several long bristwists (part braid, part twist) that she fashioned.

He looked in the mirror and nodded. "Thanks. When my hand's better I'll return the favor."

Never in a million years.

28

KEEDEN TOLD himself he wouldn't think about Maya's date with Bryant.

He wouldn't think about Maya and Bryant together at the concert or alone on their ride home. He wouldn't keep checking the clock and calculating when the concert would likely end and when they should be home. He wouldn't obsess when his calculation proved off by over an hour.

He wouldn't imagine where they might have gone together afterwards. He wouldn't think about what outfit Maya had chosen, (he'd made sure to be out of sight when they left) and the look on her face when Bryant complimented her, which he would.

He wouldn't think about coming up with an excuse to text them. He wouldn't delete an unsent text five times. Instead he'd read something and when that didn't work, he texted Amata but that didn't distract him long enough so he'd watch something and when that didn't work he'd go on a short walk.

And on that walk he'd make sure not to remember the sweet torturous feel of Maya's fingers on his scalp, the soft give of her breasts pressed against his back. He'd taken a risk asking her to wash his hair, letting his mind imagine what other things she could do with the shower hose, and hadn't regretted a thing.

Friends.

They were now friends. He could settle for that.

Friendship was good. Solid. Important. He didn't have many friends. He didn't let people get close to him.

He'd let her get close.

A little too close. But that was okay because she was good for him. He didn't feel as lost and restless as he had for months. Her help with his project made him feel creative again and not like someone just going through the motions.

She deserved to be happy. He wanted her to be happy.

So he didn't care that his short walk eventually stretched to over two miles so that by the time he returned home and saw Bryant's jeep in the drive he felt relieved because then he'd look like he'd been busy and not waiting around for them.

Keeden walked to the front door then realized he'd forgotten his keys. He swore and rang the doorbell. The door swung open and he prepared himself to plaster on a neutral expression and ask Bryant or Maya or both of them, how their date went. Instead two pairs of dark, angry eyes faced him.

He cautiously stepped into the foyer.

Maya spun away and ran upstairs. Bryant didn't move.

Keeden closed the door behind him. "What's wrong?"

Bryant's brows shot up. "What's wrong? We were about to go out and search for you."

"Why would you do that?"

"Because we thought you might have been abducted. Don't smile, I'm serious. We return home and the first thing we notice is that the patio door isn't locked. Then on the counter you've left your keys and your phone. We thought nothing of it until we realized you'd also left your shoes."

Keeden looked down at his feet. He hadn't even noticed he'd cut himself and had left bloody footprints.

Maya came back down the stairs carrying a first-aid kit. She gave it to Bryant. "Make sure to clean the wound and don't let him argue with you." She shot Keeden a withering glance. "Or he'll have to deal with me." She turned and disappeared back upstairs.

Keeden looked at Bryant considering it a much better choice.

"Sorry I scared you, but I don't need your help—"

His words were cut by his shout of outrage when Bryant lifted him up and tossed him over his shoulder.

Keeden called him a host of foul names until he was dropped on a chair in the kitchen.

Keeden grabbed the front of Bryant's shirt, forcing him to meet his angry gaze. "You'd better not close your eyes tonight because the moment you do—"

Bryant slapped his hand away as if Keeden were an annoying mosquito, making Keeden wish he had the use of his dominant hand. He hated being at a disadvantage but he knew the cast was only one thing. Bryant beat him in other aspects to.

Keeden began to stand. "I said I don't need—"

Bryant pushed him back down and opened up the first aid kit. "You're not dripping anymore blood through the house."

"I won't. I can do it on my own."

"Remember when you sliced through your hand using the chisel?"

It hadn't been a chisel. It had been a curved carving knife and it wasn't something he could easily forget. Keeden still vividly remembered what had happened nearly fifteen years ago at a shared art space in Greenwich Village. He remembered someone shouting and Bryant helping him stem the bleeding and catching him when he collapsed from the loss of blood.

He ended up getting stitches and having a mini meltdown trying to figure out how he was going to pay his medical bills (he had insurance but the co-pay was high), explain his accident to his father who still didn't believe in what he was trying to achieve and the thought of never being able to grip his work tools again.

It hadn't been one of his proudest moments. But Bryant had been there and had gotten him through it. That was the problem with friends: They knew too much about you. They knew your humiliating moments. "This is different."

Bryant nodded and began to clean the wound. There were several cuts and bruises on both feet, but a major gash on one foot. "Yeah, a woman wasn't involved then."

"What?"

"But this is one way to get her attention."

"I don't know what you're talking about. I just went for a walk."

"With the intention of imitating a crazy artist or a well dressed homeless person? I hope nobody recognized you."

"I wasn't...thinking. I'm sorry I worried you."

Bryant applied disinfectant. "Nothing happened today. We're just friends."

Keeden tried to pretend it didn't sting. "I didn't ask."

"You don't need to." Bryant looked up at him. "I know how you feel about her."

"What about you?" Keeden countered. "You don't use your 'concert tickets from a friend' story with anybody. You like her."

Bryant shook his head. "Not as much as you."

Keeden glanced down at his cast. His friend knew him too well for him to lie. "How she feels about you matters more."

Bryant released a heavy sigh. "It's not what you think."

Keeden swore. It was exactly what he *knew*. He was beginning to get tired of his friend pretending not to notice how much Maya liked him, how she looked at him. Keeden had seen it for *years*. But he felt too tired to argue.

"You should apologize," Bryant said.

"Look, I've got a lot on my mind. It's not like I did this on purpose."

Bryant grabbed Keeden's cell phone from the counter and handed it to him. "Check your messages."

He did and swore as he stared at the string of messages from Maya.

"Fine, I'll apologize later."

Bryant quickly bandaged Keeden's foot. "You'll apologize now."

"You can apologize for me."

Bryant rose to his feet. "I told you I'd only do it once." He snapped the kit closed. "This time you're on your own."

29

ONE THING most people didn't see behind Bryant's brown eyes and warm smile was that he could be a ruthless bastard.

He didn't even show an ounce of sympathy as Keeden walked (with an exaggerated limp of course) to the entryway of the kitchen. Keeden glared at his friend. "Sometimes I really hate you."

Bryant blew him a kiss.

Keeden sighed and limped his way to Maya's bedroom door. He lightly knocked half hoping she'd tell him to go away or pretend to be sleeping, instead she said, "Come in."

He opened the door and was assaulted by the sweet scent of cherry sorbet and arms linking around his waist.

"You irresponsible, arrogant, idiot."

Maya was the only woman who could insult him and make him like it.

"I was so worried," she said, not letting him go.

Keeden was too stunned to move but when she began to pull away his arms wrapped around her—hugging her back, holding her close. Probably too close but he didn't care. "I'm sorry."

"Come and sit down. I'm so angry at you." She glanced down at his bandaged foot. "I knew Bryant would do a better job than I would. I'd wrap it as tight as a tourniquet."

"I didn't mean—"

"I know."

"You do?"

"I understand but it doesn't make me feel any better. You've been acting distracted lately and I think I know why."

His heart pounded, an icy knot formed in his stomach. Had he been that obvious? "Hmm."

"You're afraid about when the cast comes off. Don't get upset, but Bryant told me about the chisel incident."

It was a curved carving knife! "Hmm."

"Bryant told me the thought of having the cast removed is stressful for you."

"Hmm."

"But it's over a month away, your project is on schedule. One little break won't change that."

Keeden frowned. "Are you trying to be funny?"

"Funny?"

"One little break."

Maya thought for a moment then realized her error. "No, I wasn't referring to your fracture. I meant the time off from working. That kind of break."

He knew that but had wanted to tease her. "I see." He hung his head. "I-I hope I didn't ruin your evening."

"You did. The concert was fine—the weather was perfect— and then we decided to pick up something afterwards and Bryant called to see if we could get you something. You didn't reply so I left a message then a text then another text then we both began to worry and we came home and saw the door was open and I started to think something had happened to you and if it had everyone would blame me because I'm always blamed and—"

Keeden cut her off with a hug of his own. It was her fault she'd started it. If she hadn't hugged him first, he'd never embrace her like this.

In spite of the rushed words and rambling sentence he could hear the worry in her voice.

She really did care. He wasn't sure he'd ever get used to it.

"I'm sorry," he said, knowing holding her this close was dangerous but it was better than kissing her, which was what he really wanted to do. He hadn't meant to ruin her date. He hadn't tried to sabotage anything. He wanted her to be happy.

Didn't he?

He wasn't so sure as he continued to hold her in his embrace, surprised she hadn't pulled away. She smelled so good, felt so warm and soft and—he swore. He jumped to his feet then felt like he'd stepped on a nail and fell back down, squeezing his eyes shut. "Sweet baby jesusssss." He'd forgotten his foot injury.

"Do you need me to help you to your room?"

"No, I feel like enough of a fool."

"Nothing wrong with asking for help."

He stood, gingerly. "I'm fine. Really." He sighed. "I'm sorry I ruined your evening."

"You didn't completely ruin it. It'd have been completely ruined if we'd found your body left by..."

She couldn't finish and by the stark look of horror that crossed her face Keeden didn't need her to. He got a glimpse of her true fear and could imagine the moments of anguish she'd faced worried about him.

Him.

He hadn't made her cry, but he'd managed to hurt her again.

"Idiot," he said with affection. "I'm tougher than I look, remember?"

Maya pulled a face, all remembered fear now gone. "Irritating mosquito."

Keeden grinned glad her mood had lifted. "Exactly. I live to torment you."

He left the room, leaving Maya to collapse on the bed feeling as if her body would set the sheets ablaze. She fanned herself. Her body shouldn't feel this hot.

She hadn't meant to hug him. She'd been so furious that when he knocked on the door she had choice words to say, but then she saw his face.

He looked devastated and lost and filled with regret. She couldn't stop herself. She rushed across the room and hugged him. Because she had been worried and was relieved he was okay. And although she'd been angry at him, wanting to shout curses at him...at that moment...

She just wanted to hold him.

She had meant to hug him as a friend, but...oh...when he wrapped his arms around her he could have held her in his arms forever.

But she couldn't understand the sadness in his eyes. Did he really feel responsible for ruining her date? Did he really want her to be with Bryant that much? Didn't he feel anything for her?

Maya sat up. What was she thinking? Of course he didn't. This was Keeden Adesina of all people! She was lucky they were even friends. He'd never see her as a romantic interest. She didn't even know if he had romantic interests. His work was his true passion and he made no apologizes for it.

She'd made herself a laughingstock for years mooning over

Bryant, falling for Keeden would be reputational suicide. Bryant seemed to like her.

And she liked him.

She was not falling for Keeden.

She couldn't. It would ruin everything.

30

———

The spies came in twos.

The first set of spies arrived unannounced after the first week Maya started working for Keeden. They came in the form of Maya's cousin Jules and Uncle Martin. Bryant greeted them then made himself scarce leaving Keeden alone with them. He decided to host them on the garden patio—one of the three designated places for guests—and treated them to refreshments.

They came under the guise of checking how he was doing but Keeden knew they were ready to write up a report on Maya.

Keeden didn't plan on giving them much.

Jules wasn't much of a problem. He was too distracted by Keeden's gardeners—a mother and daughter team of two fit professionals in jeans and T-shirts. Keeden kept losing Jules' attention every time one of them bent over. And they bent over a lot.

Martin, on the other hand, came on a mission and was prepared to fulfill it. He asked a series of banal questions such as "Isn't it hot for spring?" and "Is wearing a cast uncomfortable?" before he said, "I'd hoped to see Maya. Where is she right now?"

"In the studio."

He stood. "I'd like to talk to her."

Keeden leaned back in his seat and looked up at him. "I don't like people in my studio."

Martin sat back down. "Then can you fetch her for me?"

Keeden's tone turned cold. "I don't fetch."

Martin looked embarrassed and Keeden watched him squirm, delighting in his seniority to the younger man.

Martin bowed his head. "I-I meant no offense. I...was...I mean could you get her for me, please?"

Of course he could but he didn't feel like it. "I don't like to bother her when she's working, but I'll tell her you stopped by."

"You seem...okay," Martin said. He leaned forward and lowered his voice. "She must be causing you trouble."

Ah yes, that was what everyone wanted to know. "No."

Keeden's one word response seemed to fluster him. He leaned back and blinked rapidly. "Are you certain?"

"Quite."

"We know how difficult she can be."

"Me too."

His gaze sharpened, ready to pounce on a tasty bit of gossip. Eager to report bad news. "So there *has* been trouble."

"Yes, she comes to the studio a half hour earlier than I'm used to and is such a diligent worker she's beginning to make me look bad."

Martin nodded, failing to hide his disappointment. Keeden hid a smile.

Later, after Keeden had convinced Maya to take a break, he told her about their visit and she thanked him for keeping them away. "I hope you kept your staff hidden," she said, "If they're female, Jules will try to get in their pants." Keeden thought it best she didn't know her cousin Jules had managed to get both gardeners' numbers and had left them smiling. "Hmm."

"And did you tell Martin I was doing a good job?"

"Why would I do that?"

"Because I am."

"Do you think I'd openly compliment you? I have a reputation to uphold."

She rolled her eyes. "I forgot."

"Besides, do you really care what he thinks?"

"Not him specifically, but them—my parents, the elders, yes. It's the whole reason why I'm here." She waved her hand when he opened his mouth. "We both know why I'm really here, but the reason they came up with this idea is because they think I'm a disaster."

"True."

"You think I'm a disaster?"

"You already know what I think of you," he said ending the discussion. But at least he had managed to mollify any curiosity for awhile.

The second set of spies came the third week. Their disguise was well chosen: the Kayode sisters. Keeden had half expected one of the elders or another set of cousins. But Maya's sisters proved a savvy choice.

This time Bryant didn't greet Ava and Cat. When Mathilde opened the door, Keeden saw his friend stiffen, turn on his heel and not only make himself scarce but practically disappear for the next several hours.

Keeden suspected he knew why the sisters had that affect on him and planned to tease him later. Mathilde led the sisters to the formal living room and after a brief exchange Keeden let Maya entertain them.

An hour later, as he passed the living room to head to the

patio, he heard Cat say, "At least they haven't killed each other."

"Quiet, she might hear you."

"She's gone to the kitchen, which in this house, feels like a mile away."

Keeden continued walking not wanting to eavesdrop but stopped in his tracks when he heard Ava giggle and say, "String bean, did she ever call anybody that?"

"Ugh, you mean when she went through that crazy phase when she used to give people vegetable nicknames?"

"Not everyone," Ava said. "She didn't give Gwen one and Maya told me she only gave nicknames to people she liked."

"Yep," Cat said. "She used to call me Celery Sticks and at first I was insulted. Who wants to be compared to a root vegetable?"

"Yeah, I was Sweet Pickles."

"But string beans were her favorite. I think she told me she even wrote a poem to them when she was five. I don't think she ever called anyone that."

"Nope and she stopped eating them," Ava said.

"Yes," Cat said, "that's right! One day she couldn't get enough and the next she hated the sight of them."

"I guess her tastes changed. She stopped using nicknames too. I wonder—"

"Shh, here she comes."

But Keeden didn't move, although the sound of his pounding heart made it difficult to hear anything else.

String bean.

She'd called *him* string bean.

She only gave nicknames to people she liked.

She'd liked him back then? String bean had been an affectionate nickname? He'd thought she'd been making fun of him. Laughing at him behind his back. He'd stopped eating them and declared them the worst food in the world because every time he saw them he thought of her.

Damn his fragile ego and insecurities. He shouldn't have eavesdropped at the party back then and condemned her. He should have confronted her instead of letting a misunderstanding fester for years.

Instead he'd met her smiles and remarks with cold eyes and biting retorts. He'd cut her down with tiny slights. Deliberately.

He'd turned her from a potential friend into a rival.

And then with a well placed insult and a public humiliation he'd turned her from a rival into an enemy.

It had been a clear insult meant to hurt.

No wonder she'd eventually hated him.

He'd made her.

All because he'd hated her first for no reason.

31

———

KEEDEN LEFT the hall and stumbled like a drunken man to the patio.

His own stupidity made him feel dizzy.

He pulled out a chair from underneath the table and collapsed into it. Although the fresh spring day boasted a bright sun, he found no solace in its warmth or the flower scented air.

Everything Maya'd imagined him to be—shallow, cocky, arrogant—had been correct.

They were friends now and she'd forgiven him but it didn't make him feel any better. He'd been so wrong about her.

All this time.

He heard the scrapping of the chair against the ground and a loud sigh. He glanced to his side and saw Maya had joined him.

"Mission accomplished," she said then she smiled and that nearly broke him. Her smiles had always been genuine, even back then and he'd forced them to stop.

Keeden looked away and fastened his gaze ahead feeling too ashamed to look at her. "What do you think they'll report?"

"That you're useless without me."

He turned sharply to her.

Her smile widened. "At least that got your attention."

"Hmm." He frowned and looked away again, a longing ache of an unwanted attraction growing even more. She'd always been sincere, she'd always tried to be his friend and he'd pushed her away.

And soon after humiliating her she'd met and fallen for Bryant at a graduation party for the daughter of a mutual acquaintance. At the time Keeden had thought Maya had fallen for Bryant because he was all the things Keeden wasn't: Tall, friendly, muscular. But it had been simpler than that. She'd fallen for Bryant because he'd been nice to her. He'd smiled at her. Treated her with respect.

He was being offered a second chance. If he wasn't careful he could lose her again. "You don't need to lie to get my attention."

"I wasn't lying, I was kidding."

"You don't have to sit out here with me."

"It's okay. The flowers are far enough away." She sighed. "What's the matter? You have that look."

"What look?"

"The look that used to terrify me."

He sent her a sideward glance. He understood exactly what she meant. He'd wanted to terrify people. It was the best way to protect himself from a critical household and a world that didn't quite understand him. Inspiring fear had been a great armor. It definitely stopped bullying. "Used to?"

"Yes, although I'd never admit it in public. You used to terrify me. Every interaction with you was a battle and you'd slice me with a look before you'd stab me. Fortunately, I learned to fight back but it wasn't easy."

"And I don't terrify you anymore?" When she didn't readily reply he looked at her. "Do I?"

Maya sighed and lowered her gaze. "It's still not easy since I don't have you completely figured out."

"Maya, I—"

"But no, you don't scare me anymore." She clapped her hands as if a thought had suddenly come to her. "I know what's bothering you. It's all the visitors, isn't it? First my cousins then my sisters. You feel put upon and you have every right to but I think we'll be left alone for awhile, okay?"

Keeden shook his head. "That's not what's bothering me."

"What is it?"

I don't always like myself.

Keeden sent her a considering look. The fact that they were friends, that she'd forgiven him, was a minor miracle.

"I need another favor."

"What do you want?"

"I need you to help me try a new recipe."

String beans?

Maya stared down at the peanut chicken and string beans served on a bed of spaghetti. She and Keeden sat in the dining room since Keeden said he wanted to eat the new recipe by Louisa and not be distracted by TV.

But why did it have to have string beans?

She pointed to the plate. "This is the recipe you want me to try?"

"Yes."

"You, the string bean hater for the world?"

"Hmm. I'm trying to expand my...palate."

"Is Bryant joining us?"

"No," Keeden snapped before he sighed and said, "I didn't think to ask him. Do you want me to?"

"No, but having him here might help you."

"How?"

"I can't eat this."

"Why not?"

"Because…" She couldn't tell him that they gave her a bad memory. That she'd once thought of him as delicious and overlooked like string beans until he'd turned cold and had started to insult her while also making sure anyone who knew him was made aware of how much he *hated* string beans. Almost as if he wanted to denigrate the one thing she loved.

But it had all happened so long ago and they were friends now. And he was a friend asking a simple favor. "Because I love Louisa's cooking so I won't be unbiased," she said.

"That's fine by me."

Maya lifted her fork. The last time she'd had string beans she'd literally thrown up. The thought of Keeden and food had turned her stomach. She vowed never to touch them again.

"I won't force you," he said.

"No, I'm fine." *Please. Please let me be fine.* She took a bite and…

It was delicious. Her initial love came flooding back. Oh, it was so good. Tears of joy pricked her eyes. She'd missed them.

She was halfway through her plate when she realized Keeden hadn't touched his.

"You're not hungry?"

"I like watching you eat."

"Are you going to insert a pig reference somewhere?"

"No." He pushed the food around on his plate. "I don't really understand the appeal of string beans. I always found them sort of bland."

Her voice cracked. "Bland? They are the kind of vegetable

easily paired with others and they take on the flavoring of items around them. String beans and garlic or drizzled with cheese."

He grinned. "You really like string beans, huh?"

"I used to love them. I think when I was five I even wrote a poem to them."

"And then what happened?"

"What?"

"You said you *used* to love them."

"Oh, yes, well I found other food I guess," she said, stumbling over the words. "But this is great. You have to try it."

Keeden took a bite then looked at her and nodded. "Wonderful."

And Maya felt her cheeks burn, wondering why his gaze made her feel as if he wasn't talking about the food but rather something else.

She swallowed. "I'm glad you gave it a chance."

His gaze continued to hold hers and he said in a soft voice. "Me too."

32

___

Maya had been wrong about visitors. The third set of spies came two days later: His cousin Lena and his sister, Melody.

Bryant and Maya hosted them on the patio for the first several minutes before Keeden made a required (although very reluctant) appearance later.

He didn't remember the excuse Maya and Bryant used to excuse themselves, and take Lena with them, but soon Keeden found himself alone with an adorable cocoa colored demon.

His younger sister could be as sweet as honey or antifreeze. She had the same slight build as him, with brown highlighted permed hair professionally styled to frame her face.

Keeden casually answered her questions and hoped the report she'd give his parents and the rest of the Adesinas showed that everything was going well.

To his surprise and relief Melody kept the interrogation short and they soon said their goodbyes with her telling him she'd show herself out.

Keeden sat back pleased.

Maya returned to the patio table with a fruit plate. "Oh," she said setting the plate on the table, "she's gone already?"

"Yes. Where's Lena?"

"Bryant took her out somewhere. Said they won't be long."

Keeden nodded. He looked forward to visiting with his cousin when they returned. He grabbed a strawberry. "You didn't have to do this."

"I didn't. Mathilde did. I'm just helping her out. I wanted to eavesdrop, plus we staff have to stick together."

He glanced at her annoyed by the "staff" reference and did a double take. Something was different. "Wait!" he said when she started to turn.

She looked at him curious. "Yes?"

"Weren't you wearing earrings today?" It was an unnecessary question since she wore the earrings he'd given her nearly every day.

She self-consciously touched her ear. "Uh huh."

"Where are they now?"

She picked up the fruit plate. "I should put these back in the fridge."

"Put it down."

She did.

Keeden pinned her with a look. "Where are they?"

"Your sister took them back," Maya said avoiding his gaze. "She said that she'd forgotten them here and she hadn't left them so...Where are you going?" She followed him into the hallway. "She's probably already left by now."

But she hadn't. Melody had made it to the front door and was about to open it when Keeden said, "Don't move."

She opened the door.

"Go ahead and try me," he said in a low voice. "Take one more step."

Melody sighed, hung her head and closed the door. Then

she lifted her chin and turned and faced him. "I didn't do anything wrong. You—" She halted when he raised his hand.

Keeden turned to Maya and said softly, "I don't want you to hear this. I need you to leave us alone." He shook his head when she opened her mouth to argue. "This is not up for discussion. This is a family matter. Okay?"

She nodded and left the foyer.

He turned back to his sister and motioned for her to continue. "Go on."

"You had no right giving her my present."

"Your present?"

"Yes."

"The one you said looked strange and cheap? The one you told me to donate? That one?"

"I-I didn't say that."

"I'm paraphrasing. Your exact words were 'I'd rather wear a macaroni necklace strung by a toddler.'"

Melody waved her hands. "Never mind. I didn't mean it."

"The only reason you want them now is because of how good they look on Maya, but the truth is they'll never look as good on you. You were right. They don't suit you." He held out his hand. "And they're no longer yours."

"I changed my mind."

"Too bad."

"You can be so mean."

"It's a family trait. Come on, give them back."

Melody scowled. "I could tell everyone that she stole them."

Keeden narrowed his eyes. "You know better than to threaten me."

"I'm not threatening you. It's about jewelry. And I want them. We both know people will believe me over her."

He nodded. "Yes."

"You don't seem concerned."

"I'm not because you won't do it."

"How do you know that?"

"Because I doubt you'd want your mother to know about the Nigerian scam you fell for during your study abroad in Belgium." His sister had found herself stranded after falling for a student housing scheme run by a notorious gang. She'd called Keeden in a panic and he'd ended up rescuing her, but they'd kept the truth from their parents knowing they would demand that she return home immediately and stop her studies.

She gasped. "You promised you'd never—"

"Give me the earrings."

"You don't even like her. What's the big deal?"

"I won't ask again."

She slapped the earring into his palm. "You've changed."

"The bracelet too."

She slid it off. "It's no big deal. Nobody likes her."

"Keep your voice down."

"I don't care if she hears me. It's the truth. She's the extra Kayode everyone tolerates. Besides, you've said worse about her than I ever could and she doesn't care what people think about her."

Keeden walked past her and opened the door. "Bye." He shoved her out. "Hope I don't see you soon." He closed the door at her outraged expression.

He found Maya in the kitchen sitting at the island enjoying a small bowl of fruit. He placed the items in front of her.

She scooped them up in delight. "You got them back? I didn't think you would."

The expression on her face made it all worth it. *You've said worse about her.* Those words haunted him because Melody was right. He'd once been Maya's top critic and he'd made sure everybody knew it. He'd highlighted and skewed her every flaw.

But right now, as she beamed up at him, he couldn't think of one. "Thank you," she said.

"Hmm."

"Was she really upset?"

He shrugged and grabbed a fork.

"I'll make sure to wear them when she's not around."

He stabbed one of her cantaloupe cubes. "You'll wear them whenever and wherever you want to. They're yours. Don't let her intimidate you."

"Okay, but promise to buy her something else to make it up to her."

"No." He waved his hand when she began to protest. "I don't tell you how to deal with your sisters don't tell me how to deal with mine."

"Fair enough." She put the earrings on. "At least my sisters aren't as scary as yours."

Keeden thought of Ava and Cat and couldn't stop a smile. He and Bryant had both seen another side to the Kayode sisters on various occasions. Maya was a lot more naïve than he'd thought. "If you truly think that, you don't know your sisters very well at all."

He heard Bryant call out to them and announce he and Lena had returned. He knew it best not to say anything more before he left to greet them.

33

Of course she knew her sisters. What a strange thing to say. Maya tried not to think too much about Keeden's cryptic comment as she did some work in the studio before deciding to take another break.

Or rather to satisfy her curiosity. She was a little jealous by how much Keeden enjoyed Lena's company. It amazed Maya how quickly he relaxed around her and that Lena had managed to do what others had failed to: Get close to him.

While Maya felt lucky to call him friend she knew that at times he still kept her at arm's length. What power did Lena have that she didn't?

She was curious to see.

She found them, after what had felt like a labyrinthine search, in the kitchen, sitting at the island with sheets of paper scattered about. For this occasion Lena had chosen a mid-length curly wig.

Maya stayed hidden, occasionally peeking her head around the corner to see them. She couldn't make out their words but The Old Woman didn't look as serious as she usually did and the teenager said something that made Keeden laughed and he looked...gorgeous.

Maya soaked in the sight of the glowing warmth of his brown skin, the angular cut of his jaw, the shape of his lips. And although she was too far to see them she pictured his teasing brown eyes, possibly tender. Not on the verge of piercing someone and causing them to bleed internally.

Well miracles were bound to happen.

Keeden noticed her before she could safely duck out of view. The smile quickly disappeared and a guarded mask settled over his features.

"Don't mind me," Maya said, walking to one of the cupboards as if that had been her goal all along. "I won't be a minute and then I'll be out of your way."

She meant to grab some crackers but then stopped when she saw a piece of paper with numbers on it and a big number two. She didn't mean to be noisy (it was just lying there after all) but picked it up just to be sure. A two out of ten?

She looked up to comment then had the words frozen in her mouth by the faces in front of her. Keeden's guarded look turned predatory (he really did the terrifying look too well) and The Old Woman had the defensive teen face Maya had seen before.

She had to tread carefully. Lena meant a lot to him. She could pretend it was nothing, put the paper down, and then leave.

But she was a teacher through and through. She couldn't ignore this.

"It's okay, Jack. I won't harm Sally," Maya said, referring to Jack Skellington, the skeleton hero of *The Nightmare Before Christmas* and his love interest Sally. She pulled out a stool and took a seat. "What happened?"

"I failed," Lena said.

"Well, that's obvious—" Maya stopped short when Keeden narrowed his eyes. "What I mean is...you're a bright girl and you missed something. Fortunately, I can help you."

Lena shook her head discouraged. "I'm just bad at math. Doesn't matter. I have a make-up test tomorrow and I'm going to fail that too. No matter how hard I study nothing sticks."

"The problem is you're learning it all wrong. Too many numbers. When I was in school I drew everything."

"And counted on your fingers," Keeden said.

Maya ignored him and pointed to an equation. "See this problem here? What if we drew a grid and separated it like this?"

Visualizing math had been the only way she'd managed to make it through. She couldn't understand why after a certain grade all the fun pictures—the bushel of apples in the basket and the fish in the stream—had been replaced by lines and numbers. Her mind didn't think that way.

At first Lena resisted but as Maya slowly explained certain concepts the teenager began to get excited and tried them herself. It took her a moment to realize Keeden was also looking with interest.

Her heart lifted. Teaching was in her blood and she realized how much she missed it. She was certainly hungry if she felt pleased that Keeden wanted to try her approach with one of the problems. She patiently showed him the formula. He nodded and said, "Never saw it that way."

She helped Lena go over each problem and find out what she did wrong. When Lena or Maya didn't understand something they went online to see the explanation and then Maya would explain it in a manner Lena could grasp. At the end of nearly an hour The Old Woman was beaming.

"You should be a math teacher," Lena said.

Maya waved her hands. "Heavens no. I only know the basics. Art is my passion."

Bryant entered the kitchen. "This is where you all are."

Lena jumped down from her stool and hurried over to him. "You would not believe what Aunty Maya just taught me."

"You can tell me on the drive home."

"Okay."

"I can drive you," Keeden said.

"No," Bryant and Lena said in unison.

"I asked Bryant to take me," Lena explained.

Keeden blinked surprised. "But I usually take you and I was going to treat you—"

Lena quickly gathered her things. "It's okay, you should stay and rest."

"I don't need to rest, but if you insist, I won't argue." He turned to Maya. "Do you want to go with—"

"No," they again said in unison.

"You should stay here," Lena said to Maya. "Keep an eye on him."

Keeden frowned. "I don't need looking after. What is with you two?"

Lena zipped up her backpack and mumbled, "Sometimes you can be so clueless."

Bryant took her bag from her then they waved goodbye and left.

"Okay, that was strange," Keeden said.

"Very," Maya agreed.

Keeden studied her for a minute. "But she's right you know."

"About what?"

"Teaching math."

"Actually I'd always—" She stopped.

"What?"

"Nothing."

"No, tell me."

Maya took a cracker out of the box and chewed on it. If he was going to make fun, who cared? She'd just proven she was good at what she did. She knew how to teach.

"I'd once wanted to see how to use art to teach math. But anytime I spoke to other teachers or organizations about finding ways to blend the two, even on the fifth or six grade level, I always got push back because mathematics was supposed to be grown up and adding images somehow made it childish.

"I couldn't argue since math isn't my forte. But I always felt there was a more creative way for kids who aren't number based to interact with math. I'd even put together a proposal for an illustrated math approach and sent it to a bunch of publishing companies and got turned down."

"Let me see it."

"Why?"

"I might want to publish it."

"You won't. It's not the kind of book you'd like."

"I still want to see it."

She hesitated.

Keeden sighed. "Fine, send it to Bryant instead of me then. You can get his opinion on it."

"No, I'll let you see it. I'd rather you reject it than him."

He fell silent a moment then nodded, looking a little sad before he said, "Fair enough."

34

———

IT WAS like searching for buried treasure. Maya rummaged through the cardboard box she'd pulled out of her closet eager to find the proposal she'd been working on. She'd driven to the family house after breakfast determined to show Keeden before dinnertime.

Unfortunately, after looking through two boxes she'd come up empty and hadn't managed to leave the house before her mother discovered her.

She'd entered the room and stood over Maya like an overlord.

"Why are you here?"

"Because I'm looking for something."

She sniffed. "Must you make such a mess?"

Maya looked around the room at the tidy bed and clean desk, the only things out of place were the three boxes she'd pulled from the closet. And the two previous boxes she'd gone through were closed and lined up against the wall. "It's not a mess, Mom."

"Are things really okay over there?"

"Yes, didn't Ava and Cat tell you?" Not to mention Jules and Martin?

"They're both acting strange. Ava hasn't been out with her fiancé as much as she used to and twice Cat forgot to pick up Dad's dry cleaning."

"Tantamount to ruination."

Whack.

Maya didn't even rub the back of her head. She knew she deserved that.

"You may not care about your future, but you should care about theirs."

"Who says I don't care about my future?"

"Have you decided what you'll do when Keeden doesn't need you anymore?"

"I'll figure out something."

"You'd better. We can't have you living here forever."

"That would be a nightmare for both of us."

She dodged another whack and ended up getting hit on the shoulder. She winced but didn't rub it. "I'm sorry. I know you're worried about Ava and Cat. I'm sure it's nothing." She paused when she saw the folder she'd been searching for. She lifted it up and beamed in triumph. Success!

Her mother reached for it. "What is that?"

Maya quickly hid it in her carrying case. "A project."

"I hope you're not trying to foist your work on him. You'll only embarrass yourself."

He asked me to show him, but she wouldn't tell her mother that. She wouldn't believe her. "I won't." She stood and put the boxes away. "I'm off then."

"You can't go back empty handed." She led Maya to the kitchen and pulled out a large pot from the fridge and placed it on the counter. "Give him this."

Maya stared horrified at the sixty quart pot sitting on the counter. "Mom, I can't give him that."

"It's pepper pot stew."

"Enough to feed five giants! Do you know how big Keeden is?"

"It's to make up for how much you've inconvenienced him."

"I'm helping him," Maya mumble, going to the cupboards. "Let's find a smaller pot." Maya opened a cupboard.

Her mother slapped her hand away. "You will not diminish my apology."

"Your apology can fit in a ten quart pot."

"No, it can't."

"But I can't—"

"You can and you will." She patted the top of the pot and gestured to the fasteners on the sides. "I've sealed it tight so it won't spill."

Maya shook her head. "Keeden'll never be able to get through all this." When her mother sent her a curious look she said, "What?"

"This isn't just for Keeden. Isn't his friend staying with him too?"

"Yes."

"And don't you fancy him?"

Maya felt her cheeks burn. Ugh...even her mother knew about her crush. How could she have been so pathetically obvious? Before, she hadn't cared about others knowing, now she felt embarrassed. And how had she forgotten about Bryant? Big, wonderful Bryant. Of course he would enjoy the stew too (and consume enough to at least get a third through).

"This is why you're still single. Have you learned nothing from me? A good meal means a good woman."

"Yes, Mom." Maya lifted the large pot and groaned.

"Don't groan like that. It's unbecoming."

"I think a military tank would feel lighter."

"Only because you're short with weak arms. Cat had no trouble lifting it."

Maya glanced up at the ceiling begging for patience (rolling her eyes would most certainly have gotten her a whack on the head) before she made her way out the door.

35

———

Keeden looked up at Maya alarmed. She'd entered the studio sweating and breathing hard before she'd placed a folder in front of him.

"What's wrong with you?"

"Besides my mother and sixty quarts of stew? Nothing. Thank goodness your fridge is big enough."

"Is that supposed to make any sense?"

She rubbed her forehead. "It will later, but right now," she tapped the folder, "here you go. My idea."

"You could have sent a soft copy."

"I thought it'd be better you seeing it like this. A lot of the concepts are crudely put together and I wanted you to see it in a tangible form, how I'd want the student to interact with it."

He nodded. "Sit down. Or leave. You look ready to collapse."

"I'll leave. No I'll stay. No, I'd better—"

"Sit down and shut up."

She did and held her hands together in her lap. She could take it. She could take him hating it. It wasn't one of the beautiful coffee table books he and Bryant put together. It was simplistic.

She couldn't read his face. Why was he looking at it anyway? This was stupid. *Don't foist your ideas on him, you'll embarrass yourself.* If only her mother's word didn't feel true.

Keeden closed the folder before he said, "Let me talk to Bryant."

"WE DON'T PUBLISH other people's work," Bryant said, looking over Maya's proposal. He sat at Keeden's desk in the study while Keeden slowly walked around the room. He closed a blind even though the sun stubbornly still lingered in the sky although it was well into evening.

"I know."

"And it's not going to be a money-maker."

He closed another blind. "Hmmm."

"But you still want to publish it?"

"Yes."

Bryant shook his head. "I think we'll even lose money. The project's not in a field we're familiar with. It will take a lot of work to make it worth the effort."

"I know."

"She has a lot of ideas. Based on all the illustrations that would be involved it could take two years just to get the final product ready for publication. Even if it's not full color, printing costs are going to be worrisome."

Keeden straightened a picture frame. "I know that too."

"And that doesn't bother you?"

He sat down and faced him. "Nope."

Bryant sat back. "Fine. Tell her that we'll publish it when it's ready."

"No, you tell her," Keeden said.

Bryant leaned forward suspicious. "Why me?"

"She'll want to hear it from you."

"No, she won't. She showed it to *you* first. I think it's your opinion that matters."

Only because she expects me to reject it. "Trust me. You're going to make her smile."

MAYA DIDN'T SMILE. Instead she stared at Bryant as if he'd gotten down on one knee to propose. "You'll publish it?"

He'd found her in the studio to tell her the good news. "Yes."

"I can't believe you both agreed."

"We didn't at first."

"You had to convince him, right?"

Bryant laughed sheepishly. "Actually he had to convince me. But it didn't take long for me to come around. The ideas for this book are incredible but it will be a hard sell."

"Keeden believed in it?"

"One hundred percent, which is rare."

She frowned. "Then why isn't he the one telling me this?"

Bryant shrugged. "Who knows? He said you'd be happier hearing it from me."

A couple of weeks ago Keeden would have been right. There had been many times she'd dreamed of a moment like this. Alone with Bryant telling her how wonderful her work was, how happy he was to work with her, but something felt like it was missing. It wasn't enough. She wanted to hear what Keeden had to say. She wanted to see his face when he told her, she wanted to inhale his scent as she sat at a workstation and he bent over her to show her what he liked giving her a chance to slowly...gently... lean against his body.

She wanted to be with him. But he only saw her as a friend although her heart dangerously whispered that she wanted more. He was trying to be a good friend by having Bryant deliver the news because he still believed she cared about Bryant like she used to.

Used to?

Had she actually thought that? She used to like Bryant? But it was true. She looked at him and he hadn't changed—still handsome with a sugar sweet smile, but she no longer felt tongue-tied when she spoke to him; his face wasn't the first thing she wanted to see in the morning or the last thing at night. When he disappeared for hours on end she didn't miss him as much as when Keeden twice had to cancel their dinner routine because of work—once for his lawyer the second for his accountant.

Her heart wasn't whispering anymore, it was shouting a truth she'd been too scared to face.

She liked Keeden!

Oh God when had that happened? When had the change shifted? What was wrong with her? She'd finally convinced Keeden to be friends with her, how could she want more? How could he trust her? She'd look like a woman with a fickle heart and he didn't feel the same. Why would he? She blinked back tears.

"Did I say something wrong?" Bryant said.

"No, no you didn't." Maya wiped her eyes. "I'm just so happy I don't know what to say."

He folded his arms. "You're disappointed you're hearing this from me, aren't you?"

"No," she lied. Bryant couldn't know how she felt. No one could. "I guess I'm a little confused is all."

"I thought you would be. He should be talking to you." Bryant rubbed his chin and a sly smile touched his lips, making Maya wonder if she knew Bryant as much as she thought she did. "I have an idea."

Maya sent him a considering look. "I'm listening."

36

———

MAYA LOOKED as happy as a kid who'd just dropped their ice cream cone on the grass.

That wasn't the reaction Keeden'd expected. He'd been waiting nearly two days to see Maya's reaction to what he'd hoped would have been great news for her. Instead, she sat in the kitchen that morning looking solemn. "Did Bryant talk to you?"

"No," she said. Her eyes brightened with hope. "Is he supposed to? Have you talked about my book?"

Keeden cleared his throat unsure what to say. "He's still reviewing it."

"Can you give me a hint? What did *you* think?"

"He'll get to it soon." Keeden left the kitchen and found Bryant in the garden typing on his laptop. He stood in front of him.

"You're blocking my light," Bryant mumbled.

Keeden folded his arms. "Why haven't you told her yet?"

"Told who what?"

"You know who."

"I've been busy."

Keeden closed the laptop. "You're not busy now."

Bryant stared at him stunned. "I hadn't saved it."

"That's why auto-save is your friend. Plus you weren't really working on anything. I can tell by your keystrokes when you're just messing around."

Bryant stood and picked up the laptop. "I'll tell her tomorrow."

"It's already been two days! She needs—"

"If you're in such a hurry you tell her."

Keeden gripped his hand in frustration. "No, she doesn't want..." He sighed. "It's not the same as hearing it from you. It'll take less than two minutes. She's in the kitchen right now—"

Bryant's cell phone buzzed. He looked at the screen. "I'll tell her tomorrow, okay?" He patted Keeden on the shoulder then left.

It wasn't okay, but Keeden didn't have a choice.

Tomorrow came and went. Somehow Bryant had an errand to run and another day passed and Keeden grew anxious. He didn't like keeping Maya waiting. He knew how waiting felt. He closed the door to his study and called Bryant that night after Mathilde let him know Bryant had gone to his place to check on the renovations.

"When are you getting back?" Keeden asked him.

"Why, luv?" Bryant said. "Do you miss me?"

Keeden gritted his teeth. "You still haven't talked to Maya."

"I will."

"That's not good enough. You don't have to tell her in person. Call her, text her. Just communicate something."

"I'll get to it."

"You're avoiding this on purpose."

"Ahh..." Bryant said sounding pleased. "You're finally

catching on. It's your project you should tell her. I know you're dying to."

Keeden took a deep breath to control his temper. "You don't understand. She wants—"

"Sor-ry, you...break...ing up. I...ta-lk late..." The phone disconnected. Keeden marched into the kitchen and swung open the fridge to get something but he looked inside and couldn't decide what to grab so he slammed it closed.

Threats. If he had to resort to threats he would.

Keeden pulled out his cell phone, but then lost his grasp and dropped it on the floor. He swore.

"Is something wrong?" Maya asked.

Keeden closed his eyes and silently swore. The gift he'd wanted to give her (Bryant telling her he liked her work) wouldn't happen because his friend was a sneaky, conniving jackass. He'd make it up to her another way. He picked up the phone and carefully set it on the counter.

"I...uh just spoke to Bryant and he wants to publish your book."

"Really? Is that why you were swearing?"

"No, that was because..." He searched his mind for a reason. "His phone died and he didn't get to finish all he wanted to tell me."

"Oh."

"But he loves the proposal. All your ideas. He thinks they're amazing."

Maya stared at him for a moment then a slow smile spread on her face, leaving him breathless.

He didn't dare move, not wanting to break the moment, not wanting to leave the warm gaze of her brown eyes, lit with unchecked joy. He'd made her happy. It was all he'd wanted. And he wanted to bask in her beauty and her tenderness.

"He really said that?"

Keeden nodded relieved she wasn't disappointed at him being the messenger. "He loves it. The concept, the artwork. He had to convince me because of my concerns about production costs but he won me over."

"I'm glad. What convinced you?"

I didn't need convincing. I think it's amazing. I think you're amazing. "Oh...uh his enthusiasm. There will be some color theme changes that might not work. We may have to stick with black and white and there are some structural issues that I... I mean *he* would want to go over with you. But I, I mean *he* has a number of ideas he wants to run by you."

"That sounds incredible. A dream come true. Thanks for making it happen."

"I didn't do anything."

Maya sent him a sly look. "From what Bryant said you had to work hard to get him on board."

Keeden paused. What Bryant said? "Wait, you spoke to him?"

"Yes."

His brows shot up. "You mean you knew?"

"Yes."

"All this time you knew?"

"Yes, but I wanted to hear it from you. I—wait come back here!"

Keeden marched outside to the very place he knew she hated: The garden. He stood in the heart of it.

He felt like such a fool. She hadn't really been happy at all. He hated that it hurt so much. That it mattered so much to him. He wanted to make her happy. Make her smile.

He wanted to be someone she turned to. Someone she thought she could lean on. The first person who came to mind if she was ever in trouble. But he knew she'd never see him in that light. Bryant was there for that.

Not him.

She had what she wanted. She didn't need him now. They had each other.

In his own home he was an outsider. The one place he'd constructed to feel safe, the one place where he'd felt he'd belonged no longer existed. Not as long as he had to see the budding connection between Bryant and Maya.

Maya had no trouble talking to Bryant now. She made him laugh about her mother's pepper pot stew. They'd even gone grocery shopping together at the local international market.

Neither had asked him to come along. He would have said no anyway. He didn't grocery shop. On more than one occasion he'd gotten lost at the local supermarket and couldn't find what he'd been looking for.

Bryant never had a problem. He'd helped his mother shop all the time.

Now Bryant knew things about Maya Keeden never would.

They'd toyed with him. Their deception hurt.

This time there was no mistake. She'd been laughing behind his back. But he couldn't blame her, he knew Bryant found him amusing and there was a growing bond between them. One he'd helped foster.

One he'd learned to regret.

He took a deep breath determined. He'd conquer this unwanted attraction.

He'd kill it and bury it deep. Starting today.

Pain had always been a fuel for him.

He had to get used to it. In a few weeks the cast would come off and Maya would leave. There would be no reason for her to stay. Let the countdown begin.

"Am I in the dog house?" Maya said in a quiet voice.

Keeden jumped away from her and stared. He hadn't even heard her approach. She wasn't supposed to be there. She wasn't supposed to follow him. He looked up at the sky. "Go away."

"The outhouse?"

He sighed.

"The slaughterhouse?"

He walked forward then bent down and pretended to inhale a patch of tulips. He glanced back at her and saw her visibly shiver in disgust before she took a hesitant step forward.

"It was Bryant's idea."

"Doesn't matter," he ground out between clenched teeth and he saw fear spring to her eyes and he was glad. He wanted her to be afraid. Terrified even.

He wanted her to go away. He'd said it didn't matter, but that was a lie. The truth was it mattered too much. They'd both had fun at his expense. Her expression of joy had been a mockery. He hadn't made her happy at all.

He knelt down and pretended to inspect the flowers. "Go away, Maya."

She knelt down beside him and briefly leaned against him. He felt her body tremble before she said, "I'm sorry. I didn't mean to trick you. The truth is..." She bit her lip. "I really wanted to hear it from you. Why weren't you going to tell me yourself?"

He shot her a dark look. "Why would I? Isn't your beloved Bryant the only reason you're here?"

She lowered her gaze. "He's the reason why I came, but not the reason why I stayed." She stared down at her hands. "Are we enemies again?"

Keeden sighed. He wished that was possible. "No."

"But you're still angry."

"Don't...do something like that to me again. I don't like being lied to." Or laughed at.

"I won't."

He stared up at the sky. "I didn't tell you because I thought the news would be better coming from him."

"But I didn't show it to him, I showed it to you. I wanted your opinion. We're friends now, remember?"

He watched a cloud drift pass. There were too few clouds in the sky for rain. He really wished it would rain. A downpour would be perfect. "I remember."

"I appreciate you believing in my work." Maya jumped up. "Let's go inside."

"No."

She rubbed her hands, her arms. Lifted and lowered her heels. She looked as comfortable as someone coming down with a rash.

"You don't have to stay out here," Keeden said.

"I know," she said in a tight voice.

He gazed up at her and she looked miserable as she stood in one of his favorite spots, as if repelled by everything that gave him pleasure—the sound of bees, the sight of a butterfly resting on a black-eyed Susan, the smell of rich healthy soil, the warmth of a sunny day.

He rose to his feet. He wanted to stay angry but knew he'd already forgiven her because she was there and she was sorry. However, there was something he had to know. "So, why do you hate flowers so much?"

37

———

It was moments like these when Maya wished she could dissolve and be absorbed into particles of air then disappear. Because these moments, moments when someone actually looked at her and cared, that made her feel as if she'd been invisible all along and suddenly she was flesh and blood and she didn't know what to do about it.

Her hatred of flowers had been dismissed so often she wasn't sure she wanted to trust anyone with her reasons. But...but she owed Keeden. She'd hurt him and if the price was a little humiliation to save a friendship that had grown dear to her, she'd do it.

"It's okay," Keeden said in a gentle voice. "Take your time."

It was that tenderness that almost broke her. She felt the stinging of tears and briefly remembered the sight of her grandmother's wide brimmed hat as a hot July sun beat down during her seventh summer, a wonderful year.

Maya remembered the feel of a cold can of lemonade she'd gotten from the fridge to give to her.

She remembered running to her grandmother with the can

outstretched because she'd heard of people dying in heat and her grandmother was old and she didn't want her to die. Her grandmother had turned to her and smiled and said, "Don't rush. It's okay. I'm not going anywhere."

And it hurt because she did go. Seven years later she left her all alone. The one person who never looked at her as if she were a disappointment, as if she didn't belong. She'd truly shown her what love was.

Maya hugged herself. "I'll tell you, but I can't do it here."

Keeden nodded and motioned towards the house. "Okay, let's go."

She followed him into the studio. She didn't know how he knew she needed to be there, but it felt like the right place to be. She felt some of the pain ebb and a new courage filled her. She settled on the couch and picked up a sketch pad and pencil and began to sketch her memory of her grandmother's hat. It was easier not to look at him.

"Flowers have always meant sadness or loss to me."

She told him about her grandmother and her best friend's betrayal. She didn't tell him about her mother's boyfriends. It was too soon for that and she wasn't sure she ever wanted to tell anyone about her mother's past. Her mother was a new woman now, respected and refined, Keeden may not even believe her and Maya didn't want to risk it.

Instead, she told him about the humiliation of the bouquet toss and the mix up with the funeral flowers.

She soon ran out of things to say and waited for him to tell her that they were all coincidences. That the flowers had nothing to do with the pain of her life. But he didn't say anything.

He was so quiet she wondered if he'd fallen asleep, but when she finally lifted her gaze to look at the man sitting beside her, she saw he was staring at her in a way he never had before.

"I'm sorry," he said, his deep tone embracing her like the warmth of a blanket.

Two words. That's all she needed to hear. I'm sorry. I'm sorry those things happened to you. I'm sorry they still hurt. I'm sorry flowers remind you of those terrible times. I'm sorry you've suffered.

Maya sniffed and wiped her eyes. "You're supposed to tell me I'm crazy."

"Well, you already know that."

She smiled. "Thank you."

"There's nothing to thank me for. All I did was listen."

"That's more than most."

"What do you like instead?"

"Instead?"

Keeden cleared his throat and let his gaze drift to the window. "If someone wanted to give you something, but not flowers, what would you like it to be?"

She hesitated.

"Come on tell me."

"A hug."

"A hug?"

"Yes. People rarely hug me. It's stupid I know, but when my grandmother died nobody comforted me. I was hustled into a new life and expected to adjust. When my former best friend later betrayed me I was expected to get over it. My friends let me bitch but nobody...it's silly."

He stood. "Well, we have to remedy that."

"What?"

He motioned her forward. "Come on."

She stared at him.

"You're really not going to come to me?"

"You're serious?"

He held out his hand. "It's not like we haven't hugged before."

That was true, but those ones had been different.

She took his hand and let him help her to her feet. "Have your bruises healed?"

He drew her close. "More than yours have."

Keeden embraced her and Maya closed her eyes and suddenly she was fourteen again and listening to the whispers. Some hinting that the stress of looking after her had been too much, blaming her for her grandmother's passing. Then she was twenty-four and overhearing another say that Maya's former friend had used her the entire time. Her throat choked with tears, her body shook, but she didn't cry. She wouldn't cry. She took a deep breath. Held him closer, her heart hammering in her chest. He made a low noise in his throat.

Maya drew back alarmed. "I'm hurting you."

Keeden shook his head and pulled her close again. "You're not hurting me. It's okay."

"But you—"

"It's okay."

She bit her lip. "Thank you for this."

"My hugs are even better without a cast."

"I'll remember that."

He held her tighter then whispered three words she never imagined she'd hear from him.

38

"I'm truly sorry."

For a moment, shock left her breathless. He didn't need to tell her why he was sorry. She knew it was the reason she'd hated him for all these years. She didn't want to hear the words, to remember the reason.

She pulled away and forced a smile. They'd come so far it was best to leave things in the past. "It's okay."

"No, it's not okay. What I said wasn't true. I said it to hurt you."

"You succeeded."

"And I regret that."

He was cutting her open. Why was he doing this? "Keeden, don't—"

He took her hand and it felt as tender as a kiss. "A friend admits when he's wrong. I was wrong."

Tears burned behind her eyes but she wouldn't let them fall.

It had been a public humiliation. *Those who can, do. Those who can't, teach.* He'd relegated her to second class citizenry in the art world. She was nothing, nobody. Her family never treated her the same again. She was just a failed artist. Never a true one. A true artist made a living from their art.

"You're a wonderful teacher. I wish I'd had a teacher like you. I had one professor who tried to discourage me every chance she got. She hated my work. She belittled me. I had another who refused to teach me. I still showed up but I got no credits for the class. I wasn't sure I'd make it.

"Another tried to make me use what he liked to call 'my roots.' He didn't understand why everything I did didn't have an 'African' feel. As if that was the only kind of art I could or should produce. Didn't matter that I considered myself a citizen of the world, that I enjoyed the works of many diverse artists, that I gained inspiration from European artists as much as African, Asian and American ones.

"I fought not to be pigeonholed. It was a struggle in the early years to get people to take my work seriously but I managed. I had to believe in myself. But to have a teacher who'd believed in me would have been nice. I didn't meet someone like you until much later."

"I'm not a real artist like you."

He shrugged. "What's a real artist anyway? You're a maker of souls. You mold minds. Our lives can be works of art. But even if I were not being philosophical, the way you've been able to help me, showed me the kind of artist you are.

"I am impressed with your work and your vision. I couldn't have gone as far on my project without your skill with carving and your ideas for the book showed me what you're capable of. But don't let my opinion matter too much, yours must matter more. If you want to create, do it. Don't seek permission or validation. That puts someone else in control." He looked around the room. "I created this studio, a place where I could fail, where I could try and experiment safely. I want you to be kind to yourself. Kinder.

"As a friend I tell you this, you are one of the best artists I know. Not only do you have skill but the ability to help others, that's a rare gift. You don't have to take away from someone else to feel whole yourself. In the arts that's rare. Everyone wants to prove and show their genius."

He released her hand. "I was stuck before you..." He lifted his cast. "Before this. But the weeks I've spent with you have changed all that and I realize I never should have said what I said to you." He rubbed his nose. "I'd wanted to hurt you because I thought you were making fun of me."

"Why would you think that?"

He hung his head. "Because I was stupid and insecure and couldn't believe you really liked me when so few people did." He held up his hand. "It's embarrassing enough to admit, please don't ask me to say more."

But Maya couldn't let it drop. "Is it because I thought you were wearing makeup? I really didn't know a guy's eyelashes could be so dark and thick."

"Leave it, Maya."

She pulled a face. "But I'm curious."

"Too bad." He left the studio.

She followed him down the hall. "But I must have said or did something that made you think that. I was always getting into trouble for reasons I didn't know. Was it because I talked too much?"

"No."

"Because I showed you my work? Did it bug you? Few people were interested then."

"I thought your fruit prints were interesting."

Her eyes widened. "You remember them?"

"How could I forget? Back then most people couldn't stop

talking about the crazy Kayode daughter who used rags and rubbish on the walls."

"Is that what they said about me?"

He nodded.

"That wasn't true. I used old sponges, apples and potatoes to make prints on my bedroom wall because I thought they would give it character. Unfortunately, my mother didn't see it that way."

"You had more courage than I did."

"No way. Back then you'd walk into a room brimming with confidence even though you were as skinny as a toothpick. You reminded me of my favorite overlooked vegetable. The string bean."

He stopped walking.

She kept walking then realized he'd stopped and looked back at him. She gasped. Covered her mouth. Pointed at him then said, "That's it! You heard me call you a string bean?"

He lowered his head and started walking again. "I don't want to talk about it."

"And that's when you became the string bean hater of the world," she guessed, putting the pieces together.

"I never really liked them," he mumbled.

"But I loved them!"

"I didn't know that. I thought...I told you what I thought. Now can we drop it?"

Maya rushed forward and looped her arm through his. "Awww. Now you know my biggest secret."

"What?"

She sighed with a note of regret. "That I'd once adored you."

39

———

I'D ONCE ADORED YOU. Words that tore him apart. Maya'd once felt that way but didn't anymore. He'd discovered too late a chance he'd been given.

But he wouldn't dwell on it. Love wasn't in the cards for him.

Maya had gone to her room. Keeden headed for the living room then stopped when he saw Bryant napping on the couch.

He looked so peaceful.

Keeden walked over to him eager to ruin it.

He nudged his friend awake before he whispered, "Ava and Cat are here."

Bryant scrambled up and looked widely around as if Keeden had shouted *Fire!* "Where?"

Keeden laughed.

He scowled.

"You deserve it."

Bryant stood up and stretched. He wasn't going to deny it.

"Do you have a date for the gala?" Keeden said.

In two weeks they'd travel to California to attend the

annual benefit gala for the Sumpler Art Museum in Los Angeles. Both men regularly supported the museum and its commitment to arts education in South LA.

Bryant sniffed. "No, it'd be pretty last minute though. Unless I pick someone up at LAX," he flashed a shark like grin, "which isn't impossible."

"Luckily you won't have to do that."

Bryant's smile disappeared. He furrowed his brows, trying to read his friend. "I won't?"

"No, you have the perfect date."

"I do?"

Keeden slowly nodded. "Yes. You're taking Maya with you."

Bryant's voice cracked in surprise. "I am?"

Keeden sent him a hard, stony look.

Bryant recognized defeat and let his arms fall. "I am."

40

―――――

Cinderella was an ingrate.

That's how Maya felt as she gazed down at the glittering lights of LA. The annual benefit gala was hosted by a wealthy couple she'd never heard of in a mansion that seemed to stretch the entire length of a golf course. Its imposing presence rested high on a hill while its large windows offered a 180 degree view of both Downtown and Century City. The infinity pool, which likely looked serene in the daylight, appeared mysterious and mystical as it reflected the night sky.

Mystical was how everything about the sudden trip felt.

And all because she'd said "Sure."

"Sure I'll be your date," she'd told Bryant when he'd asked her. He'd smiled his brilliant smile, called her a lifesaver and then the next thing she knew she was flying first-class to California, whisked to a luxury hotel suite where she found a navy colored sleeveless, full length gown with a V-neck lace bodice, hanging on the back of the bedroom door. He'd even hired a tailor who'd made certain alterations to make sure the dress fit.

She felt like a princess as they'd arrived at the impressive mansion, Bryant handsome in a simple tux that accentuated his broad build and handsome features. The event was creative formal attire so she also saw tuxes in colors she didn't think possible. She mingled with artists, philanthropists, corporate leaders and cultural influencers.

She was living a fairy tale with the requisite Prince Charming by her side and all she could think about were vampires.

She wondered if Keeden was okay. Bryant had told her that he'd come on a later flight because he had business to attend to.

But she hadn't seen him yet. Not that it would be easy to spot anyone in this large house among a crush of people.

"Are you enjoying yourself?" Bryant asked.

"Why me?"

"Sorry?"

"You could have brought anyone with you," Maya said. "Why me?"

He turned to the window.

"Did you lose a bet?"

He looked at her surprised. "Why would you think that?"

"Because this isn't like you." She smiled. "I've gotten to know you over these past several weeks and the flight, hotel and dress doesn't seem your style. I don't think you like me that much."

Bryant shook his head before he said in a quiet voice, "Actually you're wrong. I do like you that much."

His eyes swept over her face, the sweet sting of longing heating his gaze. A tiny glow of joy swept over her. "Really?"

He grinned. "You think I'm joking?"

"But you're—Keeden told me I'm not your type."

He took her hand, pressed his lips on the back of it then his gaze fell on her lips, causing them to tingle, before lifting his soft brown eyes to her face. "You are now."

This. Couldn't. Be. Happening.

Bryant released her hand but continued to hold her gaze. "Unfortunately, I'm too late."

May blinked. "Too late?"

He didn't get a chance to reply before a figure appeared in the corner of her eye, seizing her attention. She turned and saw Keeden.

He stood in profile, surrounded by five other people listening to one of them speak. He wore one of her designed shirts, patterned using black and white with a touch of red and orange, the asymmetrical cut along his shoulders giving him a broader, taller and sexier appearance. It complemented his long, black hair and chiseled features.

Maya turned back to Bryant, having briefly forgotten he was there and even what they'd been talking about. She began to apologize but he stopped her with a shake of his head and a rueful grin. "It's okay. Go and say hello."

"No," she said suddenly feeling too shy to approach him. Here he was, Keeden Adesina, renowned artist, wealthy businessman, philanthropist. "I'm glad he's okay."

Bryant took her hand in his, warm and firm, giving her no chance of escape as he led her forward. "Come on."

41

———

HE'D LOST the ability to speak.

It had never happened before.

Keeden had been listening to Alan Kim, an artist whose Koreatown gallery was making waves, and then with a tap on his shoulder he'd turned around and the sight before him robbed him of speech.

A beautiful woman in a navy gown smiled at him and he knew who she was but...

But two days without her suddenly felt like a lifetime. He wanted to tell her how beautiful she looked, ask her about the flight, whether she liked her hotel room. He wanted to spend the rest of the evening with her. He wanted to hug her, hold her, kiss her.

But she was out of reach. A dazzling star. Part of the cosmos. She stood next to Bryant and they made an attractive pair. By the look on her face, the smile, the bright gleam in her eyes, Keeden knew he'd made Maya's dream come true. A quick glance at their clasped hands told him all he needed to know.

He was desperately, achingly in love with her.

And she loved someone else.

A good man. His best friend.

It made the pain more acute. He would not interfere. He'd keep his feelings to himself.

"I was wondering when you'd get here," Maya said. "The shirt looks great on you."

He nodded.

Worry entered her gaze. "Is something wrong?"

He shook his head. His mouth still refused to work, his heart beat too fast and he didn't dare look at his friend. Bryant would see too much. His friend always saw too much. Keeden swallowed hard. This night was about her. He would endure anything for her. "You are beautiful."

All worry disappeared from her gaze and she looked at him as if he'd suddenly showered her in diamonds and pearls instead of a simple compliment.

Her voice caught and when she spoke the words were a little breathless. "Thank you."

She held his gaze, which she shouldn't have done because everything else melted away. When had her brown eyes become a sanctuary? A place he found peace?

The dangerous pull of desire coursed through him as well as fear. Fear that he didn't have the strength to make it through the rest of the evening without making a fool of himself.

He had to stay away. Distance was his only protection.

"How was your flight?" she asked.

"It was fine." He gave a curt bow. "Don't let me keep you. Enjoy the rest of the evening." He turned and joined another conversation not hearing a single word.

~

Maya didn't want to believe Keeden was avoiding her, but after several attempts to try to talk to him and missing her chance, she couldn't deny the truth: He wanted her away from him.

He wanted space.

She glanced at Bryant who was laughing with two recognizable women (whose reputation didn't readily come to mind, something to do with business development) and didn't feel a twinge of jealousy but when her gaze fell on Keeden she envied whoever was closest to him.

A waiter. A stylish older woman, a flashy young man. She wanted to be with him. Not to talk—just to be in his presence.

He stood with his back to her.

She saw Keeden in his full glory amongst his peers and she'd never felt so small. She watched him float through the crowd—at times noticed, many times not—just as she'd remembered he'd done when he was younger. He didn't attract attention but it followed him anyway. Some people glanced, others stared, those who approached him did so with a little caution. She couldn't blame them. He did not carry Bryant's bright light. Instead a dark edginess clung to him.

You are beautiful. The memory of his words skittered through her mind like the sweetest breeze. Not you look beautiful, but you *are* beautiful. If anyone else had said those words to her she would have thought it was flattery, but Keeden made her believe them. Believe him.

Maya tried her best to enjoy the remainder of the evening, laughing with Bryant and twice trying to talk to Keeden again but he made it clear he didn't want to talk to her. He remained polite but distant.

Reminding her of their difference in status. He the renowned artist and she...

There was no use comparing. She was just herself. She didn't need him to push her away or draw a line between them.

They were friends and friends knew what the other needed. He needed space. He found her a bit too much, too clingy and that's not how she wanted to be.

She told Bryant she had a headache and wanted to return to the hotel. He took her to the hallway where few people could see them and peppered her with questions of concerns and she reassured him it wasn't serious. When he offered to take her, she begged him to stay and told him she'd find a ride.

She turned to leave but he grabbed her hand. "What do you want me to tell Keeden?"

"Keeden?"

"What do you want me to say when he asks about you?"

Bryant truly was one of the kindest men she'd ever met. He was so caring and compassionate. Keeden would likely feel relieved to see her gone. Although she doubted the idea for the trip to LA had been his, she was grateful to Bryant for following along. He'd made so many wishes come true. "Thank you for a wonderful night," she said before she pulled him close and kissed him because she wanted to and because she knew she'd never do it again.

He let her briefly, gently hold him close and their kiss was delicious and sweet and nothing more. She released him first then said, trying her best not to sound sad, "Don't worry about Keeden. He won't ask about me."

42

It took Keeden five minutes to notice Maya was missing. Bryant had started the countdown the moment he'd returned to the main room without her.

He casually chatted with other guests before making his way to the outside bar and requesting a raspberry vodka spitzer. Keeden had an absurd ability to appear disinterested when he actually was. He could watch someone without them noticing and all night he'd been watching Maya.

And she hadn't suspected a thing. Poor Maya. She was going to get him into trouble with Keeden but he didn't mind at all. Bryant lifted the glass and took a long swallow.

And five, four, three, two, one.

"Where's Maya?"

Bryant finished his drink, made sure to put on his best neutral expression, then turned to Keeden.

"She left." He set his empty glass down, the remaining ice clinking together.

"What do you mean she left?" Keeden said in a deceptively soft voice.

Bryant tapped the side of the glass and sent the bartender a look, requesting a refill. "She wasn't feeling well."

"And you let her return alone?"

Bryant nodded "Thanks" to the bartender before he took the glass and walked along the manicured grass. "She insisted I stay."

"And you listened?"

He took a sip, trying his best not to remember the touch and taste of her lips. "She was very insistent."

"Did she eat something that didn't agree with her? Did someone say something to her? Is it the time difference?"

Bryant took another sip and hid a grin, pleased his friend was exactly where he wanted him to be. He'd force Keeden to face his true feelings. All he needed to do was apply a little pressure. "I don't know."

"How long ago did she leave?"

"I don't know."

Keeden's eyes flashed. "You don't know!"

"She got a ride and sent me this."

Bryant pulled out his cell phone and held it up.

Keeden blinked at the smiley emoji. "What does that mean?"

Bryant tucked the phone away. "It means she's fine."

"She could be lying."

Time to apply a little more pressure, topped with the tiniest lie. "You're right. There were tears in her eyes."

"She was crying?"

"But it might have been a trick of the light. I can't be sure."

"How did she sound?"

"Normal, except—" He finished his drink.

"Except what?"

"Her voice might have cracked once or twice."

Keeden stopped walking. "You're lying to me."

"But you still want to see her," Bryant said over his shoulder.

"Doesn't matter. She loves you."

Bryant turned at the sound of pain in his friend's voice. He glanced down at the glass. The vodka had not drowned the taste of her lips. He'd never known such sweetness could exist in the world. Maya had surprised him in many ways. "But I don't love her."

He lifted his gaze, forcing Keeden to see the truth of his words and also offering a challenge. "Doesn't she deserve a man who does?"

COMFY PJS, a luxury bed, ASMR video playing on her phone to soothe her, someone knocking on her hotel door.

One of those things didn't belong.

"Maya it's me," Keeden said.

Something was wrong. She heard it in his voice. He sounded concerned. Something terrible had made him leave the gala and knock on her door. What could have happened?

Maya grabbed a robe, ran to the door and swung it open.

He looked startled and unsure. Her heart constricted with fear. Keeden was rarely unsure. She pulled him inside and quickly looked him over. He looked fine—his face unmarked. All his limbs in place. That meant someone else was hurt or he had bad news. "It's going to be okay," she said before hugging him. "Just tell me what you need me to do."

He stiffened. "Why are you comforting me?"

She patted him on the back trying to soothe him. Why was he so tense? "Because you're upset."

"I'm not upset."

Okay, wrong choice of words. He was beginning to sound

agitated. She stroked his back instead, long and slow. "Fine, just tell me what happened."

He gently pushed her away and shook his head. "Don't do this to me, Maya."

"Do what? You're the one who left the party early."

He briefly closed his eyes as if gaining patience. "I'm not the only one."

"There were others?"

"I'm talking about you. Bryant told me you weren't feeling well."

He'd left the party because of her?! He'd come to see if she was okay? He'd been worried about her? She'd been the reason for the expression on his face? No, no, no this was too sweet, too adorable, too amazing to bear.

Maya swallowed, resisting the urge to hug him again. He'd spent most of the evening avoiding her and now he was here because he cared. She felt riddled with guilt.

"I'm sorry," she said, trying not to sound miserable.

"Why are you apologizing?"

"I didn't mean for you to waste your time for nothing."

His jaw twitched. "You're not nothing."

She pulled on the cuff of her robe. Friend. He was being a caring friend. That was all. Unfortunately, her heart kept forgetting that fact. "It was just a headache. I'm sorry I worried you. I sent Bryant a text."

"I saw it."

Maya frowned confused. "So you didn't need to come all this way to see how I'm doing."

Keeden held her gaze for a long moment then sighed and said, "You're right. I shouldn't have—"

"But I'm glad you did." She smiled at his surprised face. "So I got a chance to thank you."

"Thank me?"

She motioned to the room. "For all this. Plus the flight, the dress, the date. Bryant went along with everything but I knew you were the organizer."

Keeden shook his head. "No, I—"

"You can't fool me. I never told Bryant I needed a tailor for a gown. I doubt it was something he'd think of on his own." She tapped his chest. "That's all you. You made a dream come true for me."

"Then why did you leave early?"

"Because I really wasn't feeling well. I guess I was little overwhelmed."

He fell quiet then turned. "I'm glad to see you're feeling better."

He was leaving already? "You don't have to go yet."

"Yes I do," he said with an emphasis she couldn't understand. He grabbed the door handle.

He was here. She didn't want him to go. "Why?"

"Why?" he repeated as if he couldn't comprehend the word.

"Yes. Why?"

His hand fell from the door handle. He faced her, his eyes filled with passion or fury she couldn't tell which.

"Why? Because I'm in love with you and it's the worst thing that's ever happened to me."

43

KEEDEN WAS A TRUE ARTIST. A man who could open her heart and break it *at the same time.*

He loved her and he hated it?

Loving her was the worst thing that had happened to him?

And he was still talking!!! She saw his mouth move but could make no sense of the words. Didn't want to. Didn't want to hear the litany of reasons loving her was so awful. She could list them herself.

She was unremarkable.

She was presently unemployed.

She could damage his reputation.

She could...

His mouth had stopped moving. His eyes darkened with emotion. She steeled herself when he took a step towards her. He was going to hurt her again. This time he wouldn't mean to but it wouldn't matter. The pain would linger.

It would cut deeper.

She hugged herself.

He looked away and nodded. "Okay. That's your answer."

She blinked. "You'd asked me a question?"

He swore. "Yes," he said fiercely. "Haven't you heard a word I've said?"

"That you love me and it's the worst thing that's happened to you? Yes."

He stared at her in disbelief. "That's it? You didn't hear anything else after that?"

"What else is there to hear?"

"Never mind." He turned to the door.

"Are we enemies now?"

He spun around his eyes ablaze. "Do you think this is funny?"

"I never said—"

His voice rose. "How can it be okay to love a woman who's hated me for years and is in love with my best friend? Am I supposed to be happy about that? Rejoice in the fact that I'm an idiot? Running over here made no sense. But I had to see you. I don't understand the power you have over me. And yet you stand there mocking me again."

"I've never mocked you. You're doing it again. Making me out to be someone I'm not. When did I ever say I was in love with Bryant?" Maya waved her hand when he opened his mouth.

"I liked him. I had a huge crush. That was all. Why do you refuse to see how much I..." She took a deep breath. "How can I believe a word you say? I left the gala this evening because I was sick. Sick of you treating me like an associate. Avoiding every attempt I made to talk to you. You made it clear you wanted to keep your distance and that hurt.

"Don't try to make me feel guilty by coming here and confessing your love. I think you're confused. I think you've gotten so used to having me around that when I wasn't there you missed me like a piece of furniture that had been moved." She stretched her arms out to the side then let them fall.

"But here I am. Don't worry. I'm not going anywhere. Your project will be finished on time, you'll soon get your cast off and be able to create and we'll remain friends as long as no one else sees us. I don't believe you love me at all. I don't think you ever could love—"

Keeden claimed her mouth with a soul melting kiss, stealing any remaining words from her lips.

There was nothing delicious or sweet about his kiss. It captured her like a firestorm and burned away any doubt. It told her: My love is real. My love is true. My love is yours.

"I'm sorry," he whispered, his breath warm against her skin. "I kept you away tonight because—"

"I know," Maya said, finally beginning to understand him and no longer needing words. She deepened the kiss, hoping to erase any of his doubts as well.

His lips brushed her brow before he softly said, "Let's stay a couple more days."

She closed her eyes. She'd stay another week if he asked her. "Yes."

"I want to take you to The Broad and The Getty," he said, mentioning popular museums. "And Griffith Observatory. I want to walk with you in Griffith Park."

She wanted to do it all too and more.

He wrapped his arms around her then growled low in his throat.

"What is it?"

"Damn, cast. I can't hold you the way I want to."

She smiled at his frustration. "I'm not complaining." She took his free hand and led him to the bed. She gently pushed him down on it then saddled him. "Tell me if I'm too heavy."

He slid one hand up her thigh. "No. You could crush me and I wouldn't care."

She placed her hands on her hips and pretended to look offended. "Are you making fun of my size?"

Keeden's mouth softened into a smile, his heated gaze lazily scanning her body in appreciation. "How did this short, chubby thing bewitch me into loving every curvy part of her?"

Maya pulled off his shirt and flattened her hand against his chest. "I see you've healed nicely, Mr. Toothpick."

His hand slipped underneath her pajama top. "Thank you." He captured a breast in his burning palm and teased a nipple with his thumb. "I'm in good hands."

Maya couldn't manage a response, her body humming with the sensual pleasure of his coaxing voice and masterful hand. She felt her center grow moist when the same hot hand made a slow descent down her waist before it slipped underneath her pajama shorts and captured her thigh.

She bent forward to press her mouth against his.

Then her cell phone screamed.

At least that's what it felt like when it pierced the silence with a loud, insistent sound of steel drums.

She took a deep breath and regained her composure. She'd ignore it. She was not answering her phone. Tonight was too special for interruptions.

Instead she captured one of his nipples in her mouth and reveled in feeling his body tense and the sharp intake of breath. And that hot hand of his slipped over her bottom and she felt the welcome bulge of his desire. Yessss. Oh yesss.

Another scream. This time "Bella Ciao" instead of steel drums. She'd never heard that ringtone before and wondered who Keeden had assigned an Italian protest song on his contact list.

Before she could tell him to ignore the caller, he sat up with such speed she tumbled off him. He looked at her wide-eyed. "It's your mother."

She stared at him, shocked. "Why would she be calling you?"

"I don't know."

The phone continued to ring.

Maya frantically waved her hands. "Don't answer."

"I have to answer otherwise she'll call my stepmother and if I don't answer her, she'll call Bryant and if Bryant doesn't answer, my father will call and we know where that will lead."

Maya fell on her back resigned. "Fine."

Keeden cleared his throat and put on the required deferential tone. "Hi Aunty." He glanced at Maya. "No, I don't know where Maya is right now." He nodded. "Uh...huh. Sure. Yes. Yes, I'll let her know." He disconnected then swung his legs over the side of the bed.

Maya looked at him, curious, prepared to be mildly entertained. "What was that about?"

"I'll see if I can get you on an earlier flight."

Her heart fell. She'd really hoped to spend more time with him in Los Angeles. She sat up alarmed by his grave tone. "Why?"

He scrolled through his phone. "She says it's a family crisis. You need to be there."

Maya rolled her eyes. "I doubt it. She's probably overblown something."

"She sounded really anxious."

"Nothing new."

He turned to her. "She said it's about Ava."

44

———

MAYA REMEMBERED her grandmother telling her about a machine called a mangle. She'd used it as a little girl for linen and cotton cloth. With a crank of a handle, the machine would smooth sheets and clothing thanks to large rollers pressing down on them.

Maya felt as if she'd been put through a mangle—twice.

She hadn't had to cut her LA trip short, take a red-eye flight and have the "emergency family meeting" postponed twice(!) because her family needed her. Because they wanted her advice. Because they wanted to be a united front to deal with whatever trouble Ava had gotten into.

No, Maya had been called to the family house, to sit in the living room in front of her parents and sisters and brother-in-law, as a warning. The afternoon sun bathed the room in a cherry brightness it didn't deserve.

"Do you want to end up like Maya?" her mother said, motioning to Maya as if she were a piece of rotten fruit that had once been fresh.

Ava sent Maya a look of apology, but Maya didn't need it.

Usually she'd be annoyed. She was used to being insulted. To being a warning for her sisters.

But this time...

This time she was so angry she hadn't managed to say a word. She'd been ripped from the arms of a gorgeous lover and forced to sit here because her sister broke off her engagement? That was it? She hadn't killed someone? Stolen something?

They couldn't have waited until she'd returned?

"You don't know what you're giving up," her mother continued.

Only months ago Maya had felt like a failure. But not now. She'd learned so much about herself. That she still loved art, both teaching and creating it. That she had great ideas and could be creative. That she was a great friend. She may be unemployed and unmarried but that didn't define her. She was much more than her family saw. She made mistakes. Her career, with all its ups and downs, hadn't panned out the way she'd hoped but it wasn't a decision she regretted. Even helping Keeden in order to get Bryant's attention had been worth it because she discovered a man she wanted to be with. Who accepted her—flaws and all—as much as she accepted him.

"Say something!"

Maya didn't realize her mother had been speaking to her until Cat nudged her. Fortunately, she sat diagonal to her mother a safe whacking distance away.

Maya blinked surprised to see they were all staring at her. They wanted her to say something? Usually she was being told to be quiet.

She shrugged. "I have nothing to say."

"You always have something to say," Gwen sniffed.

"Tell her what a mistake she's making," her mother demanded.

"I can't do that," Maya said. "I don't think she's making one."

Her mother gasped. Gwen waved a dismissive hand—the one that coincidentally showed off her wedding ring. "Don't take advice from a jealous woman, Ava. Especially a single one. She just wants you to be as lonely and miserable as she is." Gwen rested a hand on her chest. "Relationships can be difficult but they're worth the effort. That's what commitment is all about. You'll be happy you fought to stay together instead of running away from your relationship when you look into the eyes of your children."

Their mother breathed a sigh of relief. "Yes, that. Listen to your sister."

Ava clasped her hands in her lap. "Which one?"

Everyone stared. It wasn't like Ava to talk back.

"Gwen of course."

"But I think Maya understands me more."

"Maya knows nothing!"

Maya surged to her feet. She walked over to Ava and took her hands. "One thing she knows is that she loves you and will support whatever decision you make. You don't have to live your life filling everyone else's expectation for you."

Whack! "Get out!" her mother cried. "I want you to pack the rest of your things and never step foot in this house again."

Cat and Ava jumped up. "Mom, no!"

"Sit down," their father instructed.

"It's okay," Maya said, seeing the devastation on their faces. Somehow she'd always known this moment was coming. This was why she'd left as soon as she could. It was never truly her home. She'd never truly belonged.

Maya walked out of the living room, her mother's shouts following her into the hallway.

"Don't you believe a word of her foolishness."

And up the stairs.

"She's a failure. She's a disgrace."

They even reached her bedroom before she closed the door. She gathered the rest of her things. Fortunately there wasn't much. She had put the rest in storage. She packed her boxes and took a deep breath before opening the door again.

"...and useless," her mother continued.

She blocked out the rest of her mother's rant catching bits of her stepfather and Gwen chiming in.

Finally, all her things were out of the house. She took another deep breath and slowly released it. Ever since she'd walked through those front doors she'd been treated like a disease, now she'd been purged and she wouldn't miss walking through the doors again.

Maya jumped inside her Volkswagen then drove to another street and parked. She sat there and let the tears fall.

She didn't have to pretend her mother's words didn't hurt. That her hits didn't sting.

She didn't have to pretend that she sometimes envied her half-sisters' closeness to her mother and stepfather.

She rested her head against the steering wheel. She wanted to see Keeden but not like this. She needed a few days to get herself together. She'd get a hotel room and...

Her cell phone alerted her to a text from Keeden. *Do I need to come and get you?*

She blinked at the message. *Why would you think that?*

Cat sent me a text. I heard what happened.

About Ava or me being kicked out?

You.

I don't want you to see me. I'm a mess right now. I'll see you tomorrow. I need to think a few things through.

Come home Maya.

She broke down then. Deep racking sobs gripped her. Tears of sadness and joy. She'd lost one home but had gained another.

Maya felt a renewed strength. She was worn out but not beaten. She wasn't a discarded stick floating it the ocean. She had an anchor. Someone who was there to ground her. Someone who wouldn't let her drown.

But I'll wait until you're ready. Keeden texted a few moments later. *Take your time. I'll see you tomorrow. I'll miss you.*

She wiped her eyes and started the ignition.

She wasn't going to hide away in a hotel. She wasn't going to pretend to be okay.

45

____

IF ONLY HE hadn't opened the door.

Maya had managed to get her emotions under control the entire thirty minute drive to Keeden's house. She'd practiced what she'd say to him as she locked up her car and walked up to the front door.

Then he opened it.

And looked at her with such joy and acceptance—without question (What are you doing here?) without accusation (I thought you said you were coming tomorrow?)—Maya literally fell to her knees. It had been so long since someone welcomed her home.

Keeden knelt in front of her, quietly said her name, gently touched her cheek. Maya closed her eyes and wrapped her arms around his neck. "I made it. I wasn't sure I would."

Wordlessly, he lifted her up and carried her inside. That's when she noticed something different about him. "Your cast is gone."

"Hmm."

"When?"

He kept walking.

"Put me down. You could reinjure yourself."

He sent her a look as if to say "When will you learn to stop underestimating me?" He set her down on the couch in the casual living room, where Bob Ross's "happy little trees" filled the flat screen.

She looked and saw a standing tray with a plate filled with food and guilt replaced relief. "I interrupted your dinner."

"You didn't interrupt anything. I'm glad you're here." Keeden grabbed a napkin from the tray before he sat down beside her. "What happened?" he said, dabbing her cheeks.

The action surprised her. She'd been crying? She hadn't realized she'd still been crying. She shook her head. "I can't talk about it yet."

"Okay, you don't have to."

"I'll have to figure out what to do now that you won't need me anymore. But I promise I won't become a burden to you."

He crumpled the napkin in his fist. "A burden?"

"Yes."

His jaw twitched. "I see." He stood. "Come on."

"But your food—"

"I'll get to it later."

Maya picked up the plate and said, "I'll be back in a minute," before she took it to the kitchen. Moments later she returned and said, "It's in the fridge on the third shelf when you're ready."

Keeden took her hand and led her to the hallway. "You don't have to do things like that."

"Wanna earn my keep," she said with a laugh, determined not to taint him with her unhappiness. "I can't stay here rent free and take advantage of you."

He headed up the stairs. "Take advantage of me?"

"Yes."

"So being my girlfriend isn't enough?" He turned sharply to her when her steps faltered. "Aren't you?"

"Yes, but—"

"Then it's settled." They reached the landing and when he turned right and headed down the hall her heart started to race.

"Am I really going to get to see it? Your room?"

"Hmm." He stopped and opened the door.

Maya walked into the room then burst into laughter.

Keeden nodded. "Hideous, isn't it?"

She didn't know where to rest her eyes. The room looked as if it had been swallowed by Kente cloth. The wallpaper matched the pattern of the bed sheets, another pattern choked the rug, a third pattern adorned the side chair. The side tables, painted a blood red orange, matched the drapes.

"Yes," Maya gasped, catching her breath. "What happened?"

Keeden folded his arms and said in a grim tone, "An over-priced designer recommended by an associate I'm now estranged from. They took one look at my last name and reputation and thought 'African artist' and came up with this."

"It's awful. Why haven't you gotten it changed?"

"I was going to," Keeden said in a dry tone. "Then I got hit by a car."

He sent her a pointed look.

It wasn't funny. Just the way he said it. Maya held her sides and laughed. "I'm sorry."

"You don't sound sorry."

She laughed so hard she hiccupped. "B-but I am." She stumbled out of the room and motioned for him to follow. "I'm truly sorry," she said beginning to sober. She closed the door and leaned against it, weak from laughter. "You poor thing."

"Do you really feel sorry for me?"

"Yes."

His eyes darkened and his voice dropped. "Then can I sleep with you tonight?"

46

———

SHE DIDN'T KNOW how he'd managed to do it but Keeden made her forget everything else.

The boxes in her car.

Her mother's words.

Her sister's troubles.

All that filled her mind was him. And memories of him, his lips on hers, the feel of his hands on her skin. Their night in LA when everything changed between them.

She looked into his eyes and realized she wasn't sad anymore. He'd made her laugh, he'd shared his humiliation, he'd trusted her and he'd allowed her to be happy.

Happy.

She could be happy.

Maya didn't reply to his question. Instead she ran past him towards her bedroom. Keeden laughed, the joyful sound filling the halls as well as her heart, and ran after her.

The moment they entered her room they were in each other's arms.

She stripped down faster than he did and she teased him

about it, but he didn't smile, just continued to watch her with an expression she couldn't quite read.

She didn't care, boldly pulling him close and kissing him and helping him remove the rest of his clothes. He rolled on a condom and she nodded impressed that he'd come prepared. He'd told her he'd been hopeful.

Soon they weren't speaking at all with Keeden pressing his lips against her throat then slowly trailing a warm, wet path with his tongue. "Is this okay?"

All she could do was nod. Shiver, whimper, moan as his hands and tongue explored different parts of her.

"You're shaking," she said after a few minutes.

He took a deep breath, his voice low and raw. "You're not supposed to notice that."

"Are you nervous?"

"It's been a while. I don't have sex."

Maya froze. That's not what she'd expected him to say.

They were naked. In bed. Together. His solid, hot body on top of hers, breathing hard. What had he expected to happen?

Oh no! Had she read him wrong? Was that why he'd hesitated taking off his clothes? He didn't want to sleep with her, he just didn't want to sleep in that ugly room of his. Maya squeezed her eyes shut, her face burned. "Congratulations, Keeden, you've just witnessed one of the most humiliating moments of my entire life."

"What?"

"I didn't realize you actually wanted to sleep."

He frowned. "I don't."

She stared at him. "You said you don't have sex."

"I don't. Usually." He let his hand burn a sensuous path down the length of her side. "I'm not a big fan of it."

"You don't like sex?"

His hand skimmed her stomach, his heated gaze following, making her skin tingle. "No."

What was wrong with this man? How could he admit to something like that at the same time he touched her with hands as soft as a sable brush? Daring her to focus on anything else but him.

"But I like you," he continued. "So very much and it terrifies me. There have been others, but more to pass the time than because I was interested. None made me feel the way you do. You have no idea what you do to me. How much I want this. Want you. I want you to know how much I love how you sometimes smell like peppermint and sawdust. I want you to know how much I appreciate you keeping me honest as an artist by challenging me. How much I adore that generous heart of yours that offers forgiveness to people who don't always deserve it. That you accept me here, as I am.

"Until this moment nothing has competed with my passion for my work. For art. It filled every part of my being, my mind, until you."

He held her gaze, his keen brown eyes studying her reaction and she stared back at a man she didn't completely know. But she fought not to look away, holding his gaze, meeting his silent challenge, determined not to be afraid. Determined to trust him as he was asking her to.

"So, no," he said, his voice as soft and smooth as the sheets against her skin, "I have no interest in sex, but touching you the way I've imagined for weeks, kissing you so that I can remember the taste of your mouth, holding you and showing you how I feel?" He pressed a hot kiss on her lips. "Letting you know you're a pleasure, not a burden? That makes all the difference."

The difference was pure explosive ecstasy. The difference was his slick hard entrance and the way her body constricted around him. How he made her moan aloud and his deep responding groan.

What he didn't tell her, couldn't tell her, was how much he liked how she touched him. In the past he'd been grabbed, scratched, fondled, groped but Maya's eager hands swept over his body in a way no one else had before. She caressed him. In spite of all her teasing about how slim he was, she made him feel whole, perfect for her, with nothing to prove except how he felt about her.

He liked how she whispered his name without knowing it, how her curves nestled into the contours of his body. He felt himself surrender as he'd done when he'd entered Amata's dance studio.

His lips seared her skin with mastery, power, command.

Maya wrapped her arms around him, her breasts pressed against his chest, reveling in the sweet agony of their bodies joined in rhythmic, electric harmony.

In his arms she felt like a masterpiece. But also a creator. Her wild emotions like a paintbrush painting an image of a woman she'd never allowed herself to be. She felt magnificent. No longer small. But boundless.

Free.

47

———————

MAYA WOKE UP ALONE, surprised by how cold the empty space beside her felt when she swept her hand over it. Keeden must have left a long time ago. She pulled on her pajama top before she quickly brushed her teeth and headed towards the stairs ready to find Keeden and tease him about how a great lover could have an aversion to sex.

She gripped the railing then froze at the top of the stairs when she saw Bryant.

Suddenly she realized two things: She hadn't put on her pajama bottoms and she wasn't even sure she'd put on her underwear.

Bryant grinned at the expression on her face. "Don't worry, I'm just leaving."

"You don't have to do that," Maya said, tugging at her top, hoping it covered all her important bits. She really shouldn't have forgotten she and Keeden weren't alone.

Bryant walked up the stairs, his smile still in place, not shy to send an admiring look at her bare legs. "I know. My place is finished now so..." He shrugged. "I'm only checking to make sure I didn't leave anything."

She nodded.

"Keeden's in the kitchen."

She waited until he was safely in his room before she dashed back to her bedroom, put on her panties (she had forgotten them!) and pajama bottoms and ran into the kitchen.

"I made a mistake."

Keeden and Mathilde stared back at her. Mathilde muttered something to Keeden before she offered a cheery "Good morning" then hurried out the room.

"What kind of mistake?" Keeden said with a note of caution.

"A big one."

He paused. "You think last night was a mistake?"

"No. How could you think that? Last night was wonderful. It happened this morning. I ran into Bryant wearing only...I wasn't thinking and now he knows about us."

His jaw twitched. "And that's a problem?"

"Of course! Nobody can know about us yet."

"Why not?"

"The timing is wrong." She waved her hands when he opened his mouth. "I can't explain it all right now. The point is Bryant knows."

Keeden fell silent a long moment before he quietly said, "Are you afraid of the family knowing about us or Bryant in particular?"

"Everybody."

His gaze turned guarded and cautious while his tone remained neutral, searching. "But if he was the only one to know, would that bother you?"

Maya furrowed her brows, studying his face. "Are you mad at me?"

"A little."

"Are you jealous?"

"Right now? Very."

Maya stared at him dumbfounded. "Did I sleep with the wrong man or something? Did nothing change between us last night?" She held his face between her hands. "Listen to me you daft man. I'm panicking right now because I didn't want Bryant to know about us because he might slip and tell someone. I just don't want that kind of scrutiny right now. Our relationship means too much to me and I want to protect it." She let her hands fall. "Clear?"

"Hmm." Keeden stared at the ground, folded his arms and swore.

Maya's brows shot up. "You're still mad at me."

He shook his head, refusing to look at her. "I'm mad at myself. The last time I was jealous of Bryant was senior year of high school. We'd both entered a contest. He'd won and I didn't. Actually, he won three awards that year. I think I got an honorable mention no one cared about. I felt so miserable and for a moment I despised him.

"But then he came around to my house that evening with my favorite dish and said he wanted to celebrate with the one person he trusted, and from then on I fought never to be jealous of him again. I love him and always want the best for him. He's someone I can depend on and he can depend on me. Nothing will change that. But knowing how you felt about him for years—"

Maya leaned over and kissed him then said in a low voice, "Get over it or get over me—your choice. Because if you don't, I will leave you and you'll have no one to blame but yourself."

Keeden's guarded gaze softened at the warning. "I'll get over it."

"Good."

"And there's no need to panic. He won't tell anyone. I'm sure," he said answering her silent question. "I talked to him." Keeden pointed to a plate on the table. "Eat up. We've got a long day ahead of us."

Maya sat down feeling relieved and suddenly ravenous. She lifted a slice of buttered toast. It had gone cold but she didn't care. "We do?"

"Yes."

He held up his arm. "My cast's off."

"I already noticed that."

"Then you remember what that means."

She searched her mind and came up empty. "No."

"I made you a promise."

"You did?"

He grinned. "Yes. I promised I'd wash your hair."

Maya shook her head. "No. I don't need to wash my hair."

"Yes, you do."

"Are you saying my hair is dirty?"

"I'm saying it's my chance to return the favor."

Maya bit into her toast and bitterly muttered, "My hair isn't as beautiful as yours."

Keeden flicked his hair and affected an exaggerated West African accent. "Don't you jealous me."

Maya laughed. It was hard not to be jealous of a man with hair like that and equally jealousy inspiring long lashes and full brows. Ones she had to pencil in. "I'm not letting you wash my hair."

Keeden rested his hands on his hips. "You will."

She did.

And was glad she'd surrendered.

Last night he'd helped her to forget her troubles, now he made her feel as if he was washing them away.

She'd fallen into her own ASMR video. Lulled by the

sound of his voice, the rushing of water, the sudsing of soap. But real life added the scent of mango and mint, the feel of strong, firm hands massaging her scalp. He had the hands of a wizard. She'd never had her hair and scalp tended to in such a way. He made her hair feel special. Catered to. "You don't need as much product as me," he said, "but I'm still going to deep condition it with protein."

She wasn't listening. She didn't care. He could do whatever he wanted. She'd never been taken care of this way. As a child, her mother just quickly went through the washing routine as if it were a nuisance, complaining at the texture of her hair. She'd grown up and done the same.

"You have beautiful hair."

Those words she heard. He sounded as if he meant it. She'd never had anyone tell her that before. "No, I don't—"

"Yes," Keeden said, his hands caressing the length of her hair then rubbing her scalp. "You do. You're to treat it with care from now on." He took a wide tooth comb and gently untangled a knot.

For Maya, hair washing meant tears and tangles. A fight with her hair to control it, to get it to behave. But like a seafaring adventurer who knew the seas, Keeden went with the pattern of her hair and respected it and it became malleable in his hand. She closed her eyes feeling her body relaxing, her mind drifting to a safe place.

"When's the last time you've let someone take care of you like this?"

Not since my grandmother. "I don't remember." She sighed, contented. It felt so natural and relaxing and she felt beautiful and special. "But I could get used to this."

He conditioned her hair and then they sat and watched a nature show about chipmunks where Keeden delighted in teasing her about learning more about her distant relatives.

She later decided to style her hair herself because there was a style she'd wanted to try but never felt bold enough to pull off. She braided her hair up and then let the mass of curls at the end of the braids settle on top. They weren't big bouncing curls, but soft and tight like a hand-woven fabric.

She returned to the living room and showed Keeden her hairstyle. He leaned back and spread out his arms the length of the couch as if appreciating a magnificent sight. His mouth curved with tenderness. "Like I said, beautiful."

Maya folded her arms pleased and said, "Now let's do what you've been avoiding."

48

———

She knew him too well.

He hadn't picked up a pencil, brush, pastel, chisel or any tool since the cast had been removed.

"It's going to be fine," Maya said as she stood behind him at one of the workstations in the studio.

"Don't watch me."

She pressed a hand to her chest. "But it's like witnessing my baby's first steps."

He glared at her.

She held up her hands in surrender. "Never mind." She turned.

"I didn't say you had to leave," Keeden said when she headed towards the door. He picked up a pencil, twirled it between his fingers before he set it down. "I just don't want you to watch me."

"Okay." She sat down at another workstation and began to use her pastels.

Twenty minutes later she had a drawing.

He had a blank page.

Maya walked up behind him, shoved a piece of charcoal in his hand then covered it with hers. She forced him to draw two vertical lines then a curved line underneath: A smiley face.

Keeden sighed. "How original."

"If you can do better, show me."

Of course he could do better. Keeden picked up a charcoal pencil and sketched the woodblock tools.

At first he felt uncoordinated and stiff, too aware of each movement and how long it had been. But with time he stopped worrying and let his eyes and hands do all the work and soon using light and shadow, darkness and white space, an image emerged.

He sat back. Not completely pleased—there were so many things that he needed to fix, the perspective was off, the sun had shifted and he'd caught the shadows wrong—but relieved that he could work again.

Maya walked over to him and nodded down at the sketch. "Not bad." She patted him on the back. "With some practice, you may be able to make a living at this."

He shot her a glance. A glint of humor lit his eyes. "Thank you, I'll consider it."

Maya walked back to her workstation feeling both triumphant and a little depressed. With Keeden better he wouldn't need her assistance anymore. She needed to figure out what to do with herself.

She'd realized working with him that, while she enjoyed different mediums, she wasn't a gallery artist and wasn't interested in taking commission (not that she was on that level anyway). She wanted to marry her art with education.

While Keeden easily segued into his life before her—hours in the studio, taking breaks and doing "nothing," visits with project partners, business associates and more—Maya fielded eleven more rejections to her job applications and slowly felt a growing desperation.

She called Priya and Lars to distract herself. The screaming toddler in the background when she called Priya, who was stressed about her current workload, quickly reminded Maya that things could be worse and Lars' endless talk of tenure lulled her into a meditative stupor. When Doris called her about a possible job offer for a position at a small Delaware college, before Maya could think of the logistics of a long-distance relationship, the offer fell through.

She fought a tinge of resentment. She hated being surrounded by Keeden's success when she was floundering, but his consistent support pushed those toxic emotions away. She was proud of Keeden's success and felt fortunate to have him in her life.

She had to be honest with herself, she didn't feel as if she deserved it. Her mother's words still lingered in her thoughts: Don't be an inconvenience, a nuisance. You're useless.

She'd been a great teacher. She'd loved it. Even tutoring Lena had been a joy.

But the career she'd loved didn't love her back, so if one career path wasn't working she'd have to choose another. She had considered returning to her book on finance then decided against it. Gwen would be upset Maya choose "her field" and her mother would berate her for it, plus she had little interest in it.

Over the next few days she put together an idea for a business. When she was through, she approached Keeden in the studio.

The late afternoon sun brushed against the masks on the walls, the scent of acetone filled the air. She found Keeden clearing up a workstation and felt confident bothering him since she'd timed talking to him when she knew he took a break.

She walked up to him clutching a notebook. "I have an idea."

He held out his hand stained with splotches of green and yellow pigment. "Fine let me see it."

Maya held the notebook close to her chest. "I want to show Bryant first."

He slowly blinked. He kept his tone soft though his gaze grew hard. "Why?"

"Because I know you. You'll come up with ways to make my idea work even if it won't. But Bryant will tell it to me straight. He has a better eye for business."

Keeden nodded, his gaze and voice cautious. "Bryant can be brutal when it comes to business."

"That's what I need. I wanted you to know that I'll be talking to him so you don't think I'm doing anything behind your back."

"You can at least let me have a peek."

"No."

He folded his arms. "If he makes you cry, can I key his car?"

"Absolutely not."

He sighed, feigning dejection. "Go ahead and get your heart crushed."

Maya kissed him on the cheek sensing his concern. She wanted him to know she was stronger than he thought. "Impossible," she said then winked. "How can he crush something he doesn't have?"

49

Bryant was a different man when he didn't smile.

The good-looking black man dressed in a cream colored shirt and khaki trousers sitting across from Maya in the coffee shop, quietly going through her notebook, looked like the kind of man who hid a switchblade in his sock.

She'd finished her coffee, burning her tongue in the process, while he'd let his go cold. She tried not to squirm as he reviewed her business plan for a company that designed educational products to teach math using the arts.

He closed the notebook, looked up at her and flashed one of his brightest, marshmallowy sweet smiles. "You've worked hard."

That's not what she wanted to hear. "What do you think?"

The smile didn't slip, but his gaze shifted to one of her earrings instead of her face. "Do you want my honest opinion?"

"That's why I'm here."

He leaned back, the smile fell. "You're being naïve."

His flat tone and gaze made her feel as if she'd been doused with a bucket of ice water.

Bryant shifted his shoulders with touch of regret. "You asked me for the truth, right?"

She nodded.

"Then stop looking at me as if I've drowned your kitten."

Maya blinked and fixed her features. "I'm sorry." She took a deep breath. "Tell me more. What did I do wrong?"

He tapped the notebook. "Getting this into the school system on any level will be a nightmare. It's too far out of reach for them. And that's if you're able to manufacture the products. Just looking at what you want to create, I know they will be too costly for the audience you're trying to target."

"So I shouldn't try it?"

"Not the way it is right now. There are some aspects that stand out. Let's focus on the project you're doing for our company. I want you to develop a website and start introducing some of your ideas now, so that by the time the book launches you'll have an audience you've already nurtured. I want you to focus on parents and caregivers not organizations.

"Targeting big fish have their place but not with something like this. Also, when you're creating something, think about different price points, the budget your audience will likely have to work with. A number of your ideas can be digitized so that will be a plus. The game idea is brilliant but will take a lot longer to develop."

"So...I have a chance?"

"Are you willing to do what I said?"

"Yes."

He held out his hand. "Then it's a start."

OVER THE NEXT several weeks as summer claimed its hold bringing dry thunderstorms and days hot enough to melt flip flops into the sidewalk, Maya worked on setting up a website and with Lena's help, populating it with ideas. She and Keeden developed a new routine. He worked long hours in the studio and later in his study; she at her laptop and then in the studio working on the math book and then they met for dinner and discussed the day.

Maya became so busy that her alert on her cell phone had to remind her of an upcoming housewarming she'd agreed to attend.

She considered not going. The person she'd been six months ago wasn't the person she was now.

She thought of sending the gift she'd bought and offering excuses but then she thought of Ava.

From what little she'd gathered from Cat, the broken engagement was still fodder for the rumor mill and if Maya didn't show up to be a buffer (the "true" disappointment of the Kayode daughters) then Ava would have to endure the full force of gossip and their parent's disappointment.

She didn't want that for her.

So she vaguely told Keeden she wouldn't be home Saturday afternoon and he said he was meeting with Bryant and then also had something else to do that day, so she was glad he hadn't planned anything for them.

That morning, as Maya changed her outfit for the fifth time, she geared herself to see her mother again. She was doing this for Ava. Her sister needed to know that someone was on her side. That gave Maya the strength to drive to the beautiful split level house with large pines.

She smiled at the couple, family friends who'd both met at Ava's graduation party, and congratulated them on their lovely home. She mingled surprised not to see her mother or sisters yet. Perhaps she'd come too early. However, the event wasn't running on African time (three to four hours later than the time marked on the invitation) so she felt confident she hadn't made a social faux pas.

Maya walked into the hallway then paused when she spotted a striking dark figure standing at the far end, gazing at a picture. Her heart began to race as she recognized the long hair, the angular jaw, the shirt she'd designed that accentuated his compelling appeal. She hadn't seen him wear that one before—it had small zig zag stripes that weren't too showy, long sleeves and a patterned hem.

She lived and slept with this man and yet still felt as if she didn't know him at all.

50

<hr>

What was Keeden doing here?

Maya softly swore realizing how silly her question was. Of course he would be here. Occasionally their event schedules overlapped. Why hadn't she asked him if he'd been invited?

She furtively looked around, pleased to see there was no one in sight, then rushed over to him.

"I didn't know you were coming here," she said in a low voice.

He shrugged as if to say, *I could say the same about you.*

"The shirt looks good on you."

He leaned closer and she was briefly embraced by the scent of ginger and mint. "My girlfriend designed it for me."

The way his deep voice caressed the word "girlfriend" along with the devilish glint in his eye gave her a little thrill before she mentally shook her head. Now wasn't the time for flirting.

She needed to come up with a strategy.

"This is how it will work," Maya said in a rush, knowing she didn't have much time before someone saw or possibly overheard them. If she wanted to keep their relationship secret, they had to be careful. They rarely spoke to each other at events. "You're going to ignore me and I'll ignore you. If you happen to look in my direction remember to look at me as if I'm something disgusting you've found on the bottom of your shoe and...Stop shaking your head."

"I can't look at you like that."

"Pretend."

His gaze skimmed over her yellow and blue dress and upswept hairstyle. "You look beautiful."

"Thanks," she breathed, falling into his admiring gaze. Being with him always felt so good. "I wasn't sure what to choose... wait...no... you can't say that."

Keeden slowly trailed a forefinger down the length of her arm, giving her goose bumps. "Can I do this?"

She slapped his hand away. "No." She narrowed her eyes. "And you know better than that you frustrating walking stick."

The whack came swift and hard. "Watch your mouth," her mother said. "Can you not embarrass me here?"

Maya rubbed her head and mumbled, "The stealth monster attacks."

"What?"

"Sometimes I wonder if you even like me."

Her mother kissed her teeth. "I love you. I don't have to like you."

"Even that's debatable," Maya said under her breath.

"Are you talking back to me?" She lifted her hand again.

But Maya didn't feel the impact.

She'd closed her eyes and had prepared herself for the blow, but it didn't come. Instead she heard her mother gasp. Maya pried her eyes open and saw Keeden standing over her.

"I'm so sorry," her mother said.

Keeden bowed. "Never mind, Aunty. It's my fault for

getting in the way. I need to talk to Maya about something. Will you excuse us?"

Her mother was too stunned to do anything else but nod.

Keeden took her out the front door (since most of the guests were inside or out back) and began to walk the length of the yard.

He rubbed his shoulder. "Your mother's hits are lethal."

"You didn't have to do that," Maya said, trying not to shiver at the sight of the huge hydrangea bushes, pink and purple blossoms assaulting her at every angle. "I wouldn't want anyone to get the wrong idea."

He stared straight ahead, a rueful grin touching his lips. "Like I'm in love with you or something?"

Maya felt her cheeks warm. "No, I don't want you to get hurt because of me."

He continued to rub his shoulder. "Well, love hurts."

"Stop saying that."

"I told you it made me miserable. This is one reason why. I can't stand around and watch you get—" He shook his head. "It'll making me crazy."

The scent hit her before she spotted them—large red zinnias. She wouldn't panic. She'd stay calm. "I'm used to it."

Keeden stopped and turned to her. "Really?"

Maya nodded, desperate to keep walking.

His voice softened. "Then why are there tears in your eyes?"

She blinked, swallowed. "Because there are so many flowers." And I'm scared I might lose you.

Keeden looked around him and swore. "I didn't even notice."

"It's okay. It's not the only reason." She took a deep breath a little surprised that the scent of flowers didn't disgust her as they once had. Perhaps she was getting used to them. Just like she'd gotten used to him. Maybe she didn't have to be afraid anymore. "I'm happy you're here and on my side. For the longest time it's felt like me against the world."

"Not anymore."

"Yes, I've got a giant mosquito."

"Maya!" a voice called.

She turned and saw her Aunt Florence close enough to have overheard them. Maya silently swore wondering where she'd emerged from. As a big boned woman, dressed in an outfit with more frills than a Victorian doll, she had no trouble planting her impressive frame between them. "Even now you can't be civil. You will abuse the man to his face like this?"

"No," Keeden said, his deep voice adamant, "she's not—"

"I'm so sorry, Keeden. She's taken up enough of your time."

"Actually, I don't mind it."

"What?"

"I find her amusing."

Maya stared at him and mouthed 'What are you doing?' but he sent her a dismissive glance, his expression not changing. "So you don't have to worry about me. You can leave us now."

"But-"

"It's work related."

"Oh, I see," she said looking more confused than ever. Fortunately she spotted new guests arriving in their new Porsche and hurried over to them.

Maya released a sigh of relief. "We'd better head back inside before I say something else that gets me into trouble."

But the moment they walked through the front door, into the cool of the AC, her sister Gwen spotted her and said, "Oh thank goodness. One of the waitresses felt dizzy and they need more hands. It will just be for a couple hours." She handed her the tray.

Keeden handed it back to her. "She's busy."

Gwen gestured to Maya. "But she's right there."

"She's still busy."

"But I said she'd help out."

"Apologize for being mistaken."

Gwen's eyes flashed.

Keeden blinked bored.

"Fine," she said, "I'll find Cat instead." She spun on her heel and stormed away.

Before she could thank him for his intervention, an attractive man she'd never seen before came into the foyer. He looked at her with interest and began to walk towards her, but Keeden made a low growl in his throat and sent him a look that changed his mind.

Maya grabbed his arm and led him out the front door and down to the street. If anyone was looking it'd appear they were on the verge of a fight, which was exactly how she wanted it to appear. A few yards away she released his arm and said, "What are you doing?"

"What do you mean?"

She gestured to the house. "With my sister?"

"The one who handed you a tray so that you could replace a waitress?"

"Yes."

"What was I supposed to do?"

"Nothing."

"And let you be free staff for an event you were invited to?"

Maya shrugged. "I've done it before."

"Not when I was around."

"Yes, you've seen me. I even served you once."

Keeden looked completely blank then an expression of dawning came over his face.

She couldn't stop a superior grin. "So you *do* remember?"

He shoved his hands in his pockets.

"Do you remember what you said to me?"

Keeden closed his eyes as if in pain. "Please don't repeat it."

"I won't. But you were in a very vicious mood that day. I think you compared me to a—"

"Stop or I'll kiss you where everyone can see us."

Maya sucked in her lips. It was a tempting threat but a dangerous one.

He sighed and looked at her. "I'm sorry."

"It's okay, I called you a number of choice words too."

He looked so unhappy she smiled and patted his cheek. "Relax. All is forgiven."

He didn't smile back instead his jaw twitched in annoyance. "I didn't realize you had it this bad."

"What do you mean?"

"Your family."

She made a dismissive motion with her hand. "This is nothing."

"Your mother has the hand of a boxer, your aunt treats you like you're five and your sister like a servant."

"That's normal."

"How come I never noticed how hard it was for you before?"

"Because you hated me," Maya said in a flat tone.

Keeden looked at her with an expression of such devastation, she affectionately looped her arm through his and rushed to reassure him, "and I hated you just as much. It was how things were back then."

"But not now," he said in a low voice. His eyes gazing at her in a way that made her forget that she'd ever disliked him. That she'd ever wanted him out of her sight. Now seeing his face, being with him, made her happier than she cared to admit.

"No, not now," she said a little breathless. Suddenly

wishing they were back home so that he could make good on his threat and kiss her, except without an audience.

He nodded.

She lightly touched his arm. "I don't need you standing up for me."

"But I can't watch that. It's too hard."

She unlatched his arm and headed back towards the house. The longer they were gone the more people might begin to talk. "You're blinded by your feelings for me, it's really not that bad."

"Not that bad!" He gritted his teeth. "How could anybody hit a tiny thing like you?"

"I'm short. I'm not tiny. Far from it."

He pointed to his shoulder. "I bet you your mother left a bruise. Your aunt—"

Maya held up her hands not wanting to hear the litany again. "It's bearable. It's my family and I'm use to it."

"So used to it that you were in tears when someone took your side?"

She lowered her gaze. "Don't use that against me."

He lifted her chin. "I'm not. I'm just letting you know that it's okay to admit when things aren't okay. When people hurt you whether physically or emotionally."

"If I admit that, I'm afraid I wouldn't be able to face them again. They hurt me, I ignore it and that's how the world keeps spinning. My world at least."

He bent his head. "How much longer do I have to pretend?"

"What?"

He met her gaze. "That you're not important to me."

"I don't know. Just—" She stopped and swore when she saw a dangerous potential standing in the front lawn. "We'll talk later, go inside."

"Why?"

"Because you're not going to like what you're about to see if you don't."

"Maya."

She shoved him forward. "Go. Please."

But it was too late, cousin Jules was already on them. He grinned in greeting then slapped her on the behind. "Still a well made woman."

She tried to laugh it off, as she saw Keeden's eyes turn to coal. She slapped Jules on the back. "And you're a well made man."

Jules eyes surveyed the length of her. "You're looking good. Maybe you can finally get a job."

Keeden took a menacing step forward. Maya grabbed his arm and laughed, trying not to sound frantic. "Yes, let's hope so." She shoved Keeden, hoping he'd get the hint and leave. "Don't you have somewhere to be?"

"No."

This was not going to work. Keeden was not going to be able to hold himself and there were too many landmines. The only strategy was to separate. "Fortunately, I do." She turned to her cousin. "Gwen asked me to do something for her."

Jules groaned. "Good luck with that."

"Thanks." She smiled at Keeden's frown. "Bye."

51

Keeden kept his distance from Maya but this time it was hard. He could feel his temperature rise when he saw Maya's stepfather scolding her, as she *actually* went around the house holding a tray as if she were part of the catering staff and no one noticed.

Keeden took out his cell phone and glanced at the time. In ten minutes he was leaving, he'd made his required appearance and he'd taken as much as he could stomach.

"At least try not to look bored."

Keeden tucked his phone away and looked at his father. "I'm not. I didn't expect to see you here."

"Your stepmother insisted."

"Hmm."

"Did you come here with Maya?"

"No."

"I heard word she's still staying at your place. You're a generous man, considering her own family doesn't want her."

Keeden shoved his hand in his pockets and stared at a

framed picture of a mountain. Make it five. He was leaving in five minutes.

"I've seen the way you look at her."

He turned sharply to his father, hearing the disapproval in his voice. "And?"

"There are better options. If you're going to fall for a Kayode at least choose a real one."

Keeden heard a sound, barely a whisper, but he turned around and saw Maya holding a tray. His heart sank. No not now. Please don't let her have heard him. Please.

But he saw the hurt in her eyes, the forced smile on her face. She mouthed, "It's okay," before she turned away.

He couldn't run after her, he couldn't reveal his feelings for her. He now understood why she'd wanted to keep their relationship a secret. Just a taste of the scrutiny and judgment she'd faced was enough to make him agree with her. It wasn't going to be easy for them. People would expect their relationship not to last, but that didn't scare him enough to stay silent.

He spun around to his father and said in a low voice, "Can you once support something that's important to me?"

His father sniffed. "You're not seriously considering—"

"And if I am?"

His father sent him a hard look. "You'll remind me why I stopped expecting anything better from you."

Poor Keeden. Maya resisted the urge to stay close by and assure him that his father's words wouldn't impact them. She'd long ago gotten used to being thought of as the "other" Kayode daughter.

She finally saw Ava and realized that everything that had happened before had been worth it.

Her sister truly was lucky. Nobody blamed her for anything, the broken engagement must be a misunderstanding most people thought. Ava was too sweet to do something so reckless.

Maya returned a tray to the kitchen then glanced down when she got a text from Keeden.

You are not helping to clean up.

It won't take long.

YOU ARE NOT HELPING TO CLEAN UP.

Okay. No need to shout.

Promise me.

No. But I won't. Are you okay?

<angry emoji with steam>

I'm getting ready to leave right now.

MAYA MADE it home before Keeden did, which surprised her. She sent him a text to ask him where he was but didn't receive a reply. She decided to go to her room and change into a pair of yoga pants and a large T-shirt. She left the door ajar so she could hear when Keeden returned and tried distracting herself with ASMR videos instead of worrying. And remembering the sight of zinnia's that once symbolized *thinking of absent friends.*

She didn't want to think of the flowers as a bad omen but she had a bad feeling about Keeden's absence. Was she going to lose him?

Nearly a half hour later Keeden walked through the bedroom door.

Maya jumped up and stared at him. He looked at her, cold fury etched on his face. She shivered even though she knew the anger wasn't directed at her. "Where have you been?"

He shut the door behind him. "Went for a drive," he said every word coated in ice.

"Didn't help, did it?" she guessed assuming he'd done so to ease his temper.

"No," he said, closing the distance between them. "I kept driving and driving and the more I thought about your family and my father the angrier I got." He took off his shirt, balled it up and threw it.

Maya sent a nervous look at the floor half expecting to see he'd left a dent.

"Well, let's talk about—"

"I don't feel like talking," Keeden said in a dark voice before he pulled her close and claimed her lips.

His wild, impassioned fury should have scorched her, instead it ignited her—turning her simple joy at seeing him into a pulsing, heated desire.

His hand slid under her shirt. "Can I?"

Please do. "Yes," she said, removing her shirt, amused that he was so enraged on her behalf. If this could calm him she was more than willing to help.

"They're all idiots," Keeden growled, his body covering hers as they fell back on the bed, his hot, intense desire clear in every touch. He swore. "How come they don't see you the way I do? Why don't they see how amazing you are?"

Maya could only moan in response. Keeden continued to mumble, growl, swear, but his words barely registered as she surrendered to a glorious, sensuous assault that sought to show her how precious she was to him.

He so overwhelmed her with the power of his hunger that at one point, sensing she was losing him to something bigger than both of them, a wretched longing too far out of reach, she gently pressed her palm against his chest and whispered, "Enough."

Keeden took a deep, shaky breath and swallowed, his voice hoarse with feeling when he said, "Sorry." He hesitated. "Did I hurt you?" He drew back and touched her cheek, searching her face. When she didn't readily reply he swore. "Maya, I—"

"No," she said.

She licked her lips unsure of how to tell him that being with him like this made speech difficult. The strength of his feelings for her and the power of her own unchecked desire left her mute.

She held him, not letting him pull farther away from her. She stroked his back and slowly felt the coiled tension of his muscles ease before she lightly kissed him. "It's okay."

They both lay still, their heavy breathing filling the silence. Keeden rolled onto his back. "No, it's not."

"It is when I'm with you." Maya playfully trailed a finger down his chest, hoping to improve his mood. "Feeling better now?"

He covered her hand with his and gave it a gentle squeeze. "Hmm."

Since Keeden had calmed down Maya felt comfortable approaching the topic again. "Don't worry, your father will eventually come around. But for now we'll pretend—"

"I don't want to pretend."

"But you saw what happened with my family and your dad. That was only a tiny taste."

"I don't care."

"Our families are bigger than both of us. If we just—"

"No," Keeden said firmly. "I want them to know. I'm not embarrassed by how I feel about you. If they know, then they'll leave you alone."

Hydrangeas and zinnias. The memory of their pink, purple and red petals swirled in her mind. They looked harmless, but they weren't. They signaled so much.

Fear mingled with panic. If she didn't handle this right she could lose him. She didn't want him to think he had to protect her. He couldn't do it forever and one day he'd grow weary of it. She needed time to put her business plan into action.

"I'm not ready yet."

"You'll never be ready. Time won't make this any easier."

"Yes, it will. I'm working with Bryant on my business idea and perhaps in a few months it'll gain traction and then I can prove that I deserve to be with you."

Keeden sat up taking the bed sheets with him, leaving her bare to the cool air. He stared down at her. "Prove? You don't have to prove anything. Especially not to me."

Maya gathered the sheets from him and covered herself. "I'm not talking about you."

"Or anyone," he clarified. "I want to be with you and if others can't see how amazing you are that's their problem."

She struggled to sit up then faced him. "It'll be our problem too."

"What if they already know? What if people start to suspect?"

Maya gripped the sheets, desperate to keep her hands from shaking, the panic continuing to grow. She couldn't let that happen. She bit her lip. "Bryant has an apartment. He once told me I could use it."

Keeden swore. "Bryant again? Don't you have friends of your own?"

"Most live in another state. At least his place is close enough so I can still see you. Quietly." She took a deep breath. "It wouldn't be for long, but if I'm not here it could help squash suspicions."

"So you want us sneaking around like we're doing something wrong?"

"It's a good plan."

"No, it's not."

"You're being stubborn."

"I'm being realistic. What if your business becomes a big success and your mother doesn't care? Trust me. Sometimes success can make relationships worse not better."

She heard the hurt in his tone, knew he meant his disapproving father who still withheld praise no matter how much Keeden achieved.

But Maya didn't want to be another piece of ammunition his father could use against him. She wanted to protect him from the burden of being attached to her.

As if reading her mind, he said, "And what if they never accept us? What will you do then?"

She didn't want to think about it. She had a plan that could work. It had to. Then she'd feel like his equal. "I need to do this," she said although she really wanted to say "I don't want to lose you." This separation will keep you from leaving me.

"What about me? What about what I need?"

It was a good question. One she didn't want to answer. She feared what he needed was something she couldn't give him. She rested a tentative hand on his arm, wanting to hold tight. She needed him to know how much he meant to her. "I'm doing this for both of us."

Keeden rested his head back and sighed. "Fine." But somehow his resignation sounded like "Goodbye."

52

MAYA NEVER SUSPECTED her carefully thought out plan could be destroyed with a smile and a word.

One word: No.

She stared at Bryant as he casually finished his sparkling water.

He'd agreed to meet her in a Greek restaurant where he wanted to treat her to gyros stuffed with spiced roasted chickpeas.

Although they could have met at Keeden's place since he was gone for three days. He was a guest lecturer at an artist's retreat in upstate New York.

If they hadn't argued she might have gone with him, but as things stood...

Maya set her food down unsure she'd heard correctly. Bryant quickly read her expression and nodded. "Yes, I said no."

She glanced at his peach shirt, exuding elegance and style, and the way he leaned back in his seat as if he owned the restaurant rather than being a patron in it. She felt like she was being turned down by a model for Hugo Boss apparel.

"But you said I could use your apartment."

"To get away not to hide."

"I'm not hiding. I explained it to you. It's a strategic move—"

"Don't fool yourself. You're running. You're hiding. You're being a coward."

"A coward?"

Bryant held his chin in his hand and grinned, looking as harmless as a wolf. "Did you really think I'd help you hurt my best friend?"

Maya suddenly understood her sister's words about Bryant not being everything she thought he was. The man in front of her, whose smile had once made her tongue tied, now made her tongue freeze for a completely different reason. His brown eyes shone—like the fierce gaze of a protector. She gripped her hand into a fist, prepared to fight his silent accusation. "I don't want to hurt him."

"I know you don't, that's the only reason I'm talking to you right now."

"This plan is for us."

He leaned back, folded his arms and shook his head in pity. "How unoriginal. At least admit it's for you. You're too afraid to face the ridicule. You're too afraid to really see how Keeden will react. You're scared he'll leave you so you want to leave first."

"To give me time to achieve some success."

"And if it doesn't happen? What then?"

Why did they both have to ask her that? Why didn't they believe her plan would work?

"Do you resent his success that much? Is that what this is about? You can't stomach the difference between you?"

"No."

"What do you have to offer him Maya? Without his place, you'd be homeless. You don't have a job. You're attractive enough, but your background—"

"Stop." Tears fell. "Not you too. I thought we were friends."

Bryant sat forward alarmed. He swore. "Don't cry. Keeden would kill me if..." He took her hand. "I'm only saying the things you say to yourself. Am I right?"

Maya lowered her gaze, feeling ashamed. "Is it wrong to want to be at least a little closer in status to where he is?"

Bryant leaned back and shook his head. "You won't be. Trust me I've tried. I win awards, I make money but..." He shrugged.

"At least no one questions you being with him. You have everything I lack."

Bryant pinched the back of her hand.

Maya snatched her hand away and glared at him. "That really hurt."

"Good. Stop feeling sorry for yourself." He took another sip of water. "You're beginning to bore me and you'll soon do the same to Keeden."

"Bore him?"

He nodded. "What happened to the Maya who can wear the same outfit twice and not care what others think? The one who chose a career path that suited her and not her family? The one who could verbally battle Keeden even though she's half his size, makes not even a quarter of his income and doesn't have the pedigree but doesn't care? That's the Maya I'm willing to help. Not this one."

She'd forgotten that. She'd let her mother kicking her out of the family house, Gwen's treatment at the housewarming and Keeden's father's words cause her to forget that she was already worthy.

You are my precious child, her grandmother once told her before giving Maya a hug. She'd just returned from her garden and had smelled like moist soil and gardenias.

And briefly Maya remembered the scent of mint mingling with the aroma of zinnia's as Keeden walked beside her that day at the housewarming. And she thought of other times when seeing him in his garden hadn't caused her pain—the sight of lush green leaves and the animation on his face as he talked to his gardeners, the peace his flowers gave him as he strolled along his garden deep in thought, the gentle way his hands would skim along the bushes and flowers as he checked their welfare.

What if the flowers that day at the party hadn't signaled possible loss, betrayal, despair?

What if, this time, flowers meant hope? A chance to dream? A chance to hold on to something—someone—dear to her?

She now understood why Keeden had said those words all those months ago. That falling in love with her had been the worst thing to happen to him. He wasn't being insulting, he was being honest about how he felt. More honest than she'd let herself be. Yes, falling in love was terrifying. It was incredibly scary to be so vulnerable with someone else. Someone who could leave you or fall out of love with you. Even more terrifying to face what others would say or how they'd react.

Loving was risky. But it was also wonderful. She felt a surging joy at the prospect of a bright future. One where she teased Keeden about his ugly bedroom as she helped him redesign it to make it theirs. How he challenged her with her work and forced her to stretch her skills, but most of all being in his presence because it was one of the happiest places to be.

She lifted up her gyro. "About that other Maya you're talking about."

"The one who doesn't give a damn?" Bryant nodded, his brown eyes warm and encouraging. "What about her?"

Maya grinned. "She's back."

53

---

*W*EAR *the green and black shirt.*

Keeden stared down at the text Maya had sent him. He hadn't seen her since he'd returned from New York. She'd let him know she was visiting a friend out of town and would see him tomorrow.

Keeden set the cell phone down and stared at the items in his closet. Maya knew he'd planned on attending his stepmother's sixtieth birthday party. He knew better than to ask her to come with him even though the rest of the Kayodes would be there.

Wear the green and black shirt.

He sighed and pulled down the shirt. Why did it even matter?

She'd never said she loved him.

Not once. No matter how many times he said it to her.

Maybe she didn't. Maybe he was too difficult a man to love.

Why had he let her into his sacred place? Now his studio was a reminder of loss instead of an escape.

While in New York, he'd visited Amata's dance studio and

she'd immediately sensed something was wrong. But she
wouldn't let him tell her. She had him do some routine warm
ups then said, "Show me."

He shook his head. "I'm out of practice."

"With a body like that? No you're not. Go." She put the
music on.

He didn't move.

"What's her name?" She held up a hand when he opened
his mouth. "Show me." He swayed side to side, that's how he
pictured Maya's name. "What does she mean to you?"

That proved harder to express. He stretched his arms high
then curved the air as if grabbing the world, the sky, infinity
then pulled it to his chest.

"What happened?"

That's when he felt the burning rage. He thought of the
party, her treatment by her mother, his father's words, how he'd
once treated her with contempt. Regrets assailed him. Too
many of them. Too many to overcome.

He leapt, he spun, he jumped, he rolled, he threw out his
arms then pulled them close. Then he fell to the ground
because that was what Amata had taught him—how to fall, how
to land without breaking. After the death of his mother, art had
provided a sanctuary. But now...

The pain cut too deep. Why didn't she trust him to protect
her? Why didn't she believe that together they could battle
anything? How could it be so easy for her to leave him?

She'd turned to Bryant for his business acumen.

Bryant for a place to hide. For comfort.

Not him.

Perhaps it would always be this way because of their past
animosity. Because of his mistakes. He couldn't pretend that he
hadn't been one of her tormentors. He'd been willfully blind to
what she'd had to endure.

She'd once told him Bryant didn't have her heart, but Keeden wasn't sure he had it either.

Sweat dripped from his forehead, clung to his back, his breathing grew shallow and he fought to control it otherwise he'd collapse.

He closed his eyes, feeling the full force of her rejection, the full pain of his growing fear. What if he wasn't enough? What if his love didn't matter?

He heard the sound of Amata's wheelchair come up to him, felt Amata's hand on his back. "Don't shut down. Tell her how you feel."

"She knows," he said bitterly. "I've told her everything, there's nothing left to say. She wants me to pretend. She wants me to be someone I'm not."

"Then let her go."

Keeden thought of Amata's words as he stood in the closet. He wasn't an easy man and Maya had broken down his walls. But he wouldn't build walls around her.

Instead of shutting down, locking her out, which he usually did, he wouldn't hold on. He wouldn't hurt her with his love.

He'd wear the damn shirt and then let her go.

KEEDEN STOOD in the gazebo and watched the party guests fill the garden. He'd barely spoken to his father, but Lena hadn't left his side, eager to tell him all the things Maya had taught her and how much she was helping with Maya's latest project.

Keeden didn't want to hear it, Maya was the last person he wanted to talk about, but he kept quiet because he didn't want to squash her enthusiasm.

A growing number of whispers swept through the crowd, alerting him to new arrivals. When Keeden looked up to see his stepmother's new guest he wasn't surprised to see Bryant. His friend's presence usually got people talking, but it soon became clear that the woman draped in a white shawl, standing by his side was the true reason for the whispers.

That was also nothing new. People always had an opinion about Maya Kayode.

Keeden saw the pair and his heart constricted. Maya had no trouble arriving with Bryant while shunning him.

He watched Maya turn to Bryant and say something. Bryant nodded then took her shawl and the whispers exploded into cries of shock. Amazement.

Keeden stared.

Maya beamed.

Their eyes met.

Maya looked pointedly at Keeden's shirt.

Keeden looked pointedly at Maya's dress.

It was made from the exact same fabric as his.

They looked like a couple. It was her declaration: I love you too. They no longer had to keep their relationship a secret.

A terrifying joy seized him. He hadn't lost her.

He didn't smile. Maya hadn't expected him to. He wasn't one to exuberantly express his feelings in public, but his gaze never left hers.

Lena released a girlish squeal of delight. "I knew you two would be perfect together."

Maya walked up to him, ignoring the comments and glances that followed her every step. She stopped in front of him and struck a pose, modeling her outfit. "What do you think?"

Keeden shook his head. "I don't know what to say."

She let her arms fall to her side. "In case you haven't figured it out. I love you. I decided you were right. I don't want to hide how I feel about you."

Keeden pulled her close and whispered, "I'd kiss you but I'm afraid if I did I wouldn't stop."

Maya laughed and drew away. "Good because there are people watching."

He pressed a light kiss on her forehead. "Can we at least have some flowers at our wedding?"

Maya pulled a face then released an exaggerated sigh. "Fine, but I'm not holding a bouquet."

Keeden grinned. "That's a compromise I can live with."

EPILOGUE

A YEAR LATER

MAYA SAT ALONE in the studio and grinned at the image in The Walters Arts Museum magazine. The commissioned piece she'd helped Keeden finish stood prominently in a gallery feature.

What had amused her even more had been that the magazine had been sent by her mother. Their relationship hadn't completely improved but at least Maya was no longer banned from the family home.

An unexpected side benefit of following Bryant's advice about posting her ideas about using art to teach math had led to a steady stream of income tutoring students online using her unique approach.

Bryant had helped her design two products that were already selling well while she continued to work on her larger book project. He continued to be a man full of surprises. He was not only a great friend, a savvy business partner but an even better brother-in-law.

Maya closed the magazine ready to leave the studio when

she decided to look at Keeden's special project: the illustrated story.

She sat at the workstation surprised to see panels for his story she hadn't seen before. He'd continued his story. She sat down with eagerness.

She ended up in tears.

Because in the last panel the dog had made it inside the house and was asleep on a little girl's lap. A chubby, little girl with two tightly curled puffs. A little girl that looked like the picture she'd shown him of herself with her grandmother.

And the dog with the long black fur, she knew represented him.

He'd given the dog a happy ending.

"Well?" Keeden said, coming up behind her. He rested his hand on her shoulders. "What do you think?"

"I'd make one little change."

"Really?"

"Yes." She picked up a pencil. "May I?"

He nodded.

She erased the arms which were at the child's side. She sketched them wrapped around the dog. "I think that's better. Now there's no doubt he's where he belongs."

He stared, speechless. Moved by her action.

She took his hand, the one that wore the wedding band she'd placed there, the one that matched her own. "And she's so happy," Maya said, her smile mirroring the love in her heart.

"She's not the only one," Keeden said before he kissed her and held her tight, leaving no doubt she'd found where she'd belonged as well.

ABOUT THE AUTHOR

Dara Girard, an award-winning, national bestselling author of more than fifty novels, from romance to suspense, loves telling stories.

Born in the US to immigrant parents, Dara enjoys pulling from her Jamaican, British, Nigerian heritage and exposure to various cultures to bring what reviewers and fans call "vivid emotional stories" to life. She is best known for her popular Henson Series, the mysterious Clifton Sisters, and the fun Black Stockings Society.

You can write her at:
contactdara@daragirard.com
or
P.O. Box 10345
Silver Spring, MD 20914
If you'd like to receive a reply, please send a self-addressed stamped envelope.

Visit her website to sign up for her newsletter and get sneak peeks, monthly updates on new releases, and special offers.

For more information visit
www.daragirard.com